Dear Bill

The collected letters of Denis Thatcher

Published in Great Britain by Private Eye Productions Ltd.,
34 Greek Street, London W1.
In association with Andre Deutsch Ltd.,
105 Great Russell Street, London WC1.

© 1980 Pressdram Limited.

Illustrations by George Adamson, ©1980

Designed by Peter Windett.

ISBN 233 973036

Printed by Billing & Sons Ltd.,
Walnut Tree Close,
Guildford, Surrey.

Dear Bill

The collected letters of Denis Thatcher

Written by Richard Ingrams & John Wells
Illustrated by George Adamson

PRIVATE EYE/ANDRE DEUTSCH

FROM DENIS AND MARGARET THATCHER

10 Downing Street
S. W. 1. 94 FLOOD STREET
LONDON SW3

18 MAY 1979

Dear Bill,

So sorry I couldn't make it on Tuesday. Monty rang me last
night to report, and obviously I missed a jolly good day.
I haven't played down at Sandwich since '68, when poor old
Archie Bracketts dropped down dead at the fourteenth. I
remember we drove over to the Dolphin afterwards and had a
slap-up meal, which I am sure is what Archie would have
wanted had he been alive.

Anyway, as you may have seen in the *Telegraph*, all hell
has broken loose around here since we were last able to have a
chat over lunch that day at the Army & Navy. M. has become
Prime Minister, and it's caused no end of a flap. Telephone
never stops ringing. All my daffs got trampled by a lot of
bloody pressmen on election day. I actually spotted some
photographer johnny from the *Sun* nipping up the fire-escape
trying to catch Carol starkers in the bath, dirty bugger.

To cap it all, we've now had to ship the whole shooting
match over to Number Ten, and I don't know yet whether
I'm coming or going. The bloody fools from Pickfords seem to
have lost that set of Ping Irons Burmah gave me when I
handed in my cards. What with decorators, policemen and
politicos running about all over the place, Number Ten is the
worst shambles I've seen since the Dieppe show in '42.
What's more, there doesn't seem to be a decent local, and
they've even got some Ministry of Works chappie called
Boris to take care of the garden, so any hope I had of taking
off a peaceful hour or two in the greenhouse is out of the
window.

Anyway, back to Tuesday. Why I couldn't make it was
that M. insisted I turn up for some kind of State Opening of
Parliament or other. I had assumed now the election was over
I would be excused this kind of thing, but oh no. I had just
carried my spare clubs out to the jalopy when heigh ho!
— up goes a window and M. is giving me my marching orders.

It's off to Moss Bros. for the full kit, and at that moment, I don't mind telling you, I couldn't help thinking pretty enviously of you, Monty and the Major enjoying a few pre-match snifters at the 19th without a care in the world.

It took ages to get kitted out. The staff at Moss Bros. all seem to be gyppos these days, and there was a bit of a communications problem. But eventually I managed to get a cab back to the House of Commons, only to find that I'd left my Invite back at Downing Street. I told the chap on the door that I was Mr Thatcher, and he said, "That's what they all say". After about 20 minutes they agreed to go and get M. out to vouch for my *bona fides* and, as you can imagine, I wasn't top of the popularity stakes at that particular juncture!!

M. then had to go off to do her stuff, so I just mooched

6

around for a while, looking for a watering-hole. What a place, Bill! If you ask me, it's just an antiquated rabbit warren — miles and miles of corridors, with chaps in evening dress wandering about like a lot of super-annuated penguins. Luckily I eventually bumped into a familiar face in the shape of George Brown. He seemed to know his way about, and we ended up in a nice little bar overlooking the river, with an awfully jolly crowd of chaps who were watching the show on the TV.

It all seemed to go quite smoothly, but I was a bit miffed to see M. fussing over that fellow Stevas, and taking the fluff off his collar. To tell you the truth, I don't like the cut of that chap's jib. If you ask me, he's not absolutely 100%, and when I said as much a lot of the fellows at the bar agreed.

On a more serious note, do tell Monty and the Major that I am definitely on for the 24th. I've checked with M's secretary, and there's absolutely nothing in the book. So I'll get the usual 11.08 from Charing Cross, and if Monty could pick me up at Tonbridge, we'll meet you in Ye Olde Shippe In Ye Bottle at 12.00 sharp. (I wonder if they've still got any of that Glen Keswick we had the night poor old Tuppy bought it?) Must close, as M. has got some Hun coming to dinner and I've got to do my stuff again. I sometimes wonder who won the bloody war!

Yours aye!

DENIS

1 JUNE 1979

Dear Bill,

What can you think of me? I tried desperately to get through at Ye Olde Shippe but no joy. Some foreign chappie in the kitchen who wasn't making much sense thought you'd all gone off in a charabanc to Deal, and I knew that couldn't be right. Anyway, the Major rang me next morning and I gather I missed another cracking day out at Littlestone.

As I tried to explain to the Major, who sounded rather plastered even at breakfast time (!), I got hauled in to do my stuff at HQ. It really is the most extraordinary building: looks like an ordinary house from outside, give or take a bobby on the front door, but when you get in it's just like a lot of boardrooms, very similar to the set-up at Burmah, and very difficult to find the smallest room. We're really camping on the top floor and there are endless arguments between M. and that Stevas chap about wallpaper.

Anyway, come the twenty-fourth, M. announces at breakfast that I'm on parade that evening for "bridge building". Something cold in the dining room with Ted Heath. To be perfectly frank I don't know what it was all about. Ted was supposed to bring some sort of pianist woman, but she cried off at the last minute. To put the tin hat on it, M. got tied up with her hanging bunch at the House, and rang through to me and told me to hold the fort. Ted arrived a quarter of an hour early, so yours truly was well and truly lumbered.

I took him upstairs into what they call the blue room and offered him a drink, but he refused rather huffily, saying, "Most people know I'm on a diet." He then gave me a shirty look when I helped myself to a stiff one. Then there was a deathly hush from both ends of the wicket. Finally, to break the ice, I asked him if he ever played golf. He said, "No". The hush then resumed. Then he looked at his watch and asked rather testily, "Have you any idea why that woman wants to see me?"

I was still trying to haul that one in when he looked at me in an odd sort of way and said, "Do you work here? In my day I must say we had a rather younger crew."

A pretty tricky situation, as you can imagine, Bill. Not unlike the time the Vicar mistook your good lady for the bar-maid of the Bull. Fortunately young Cosgrove got us off the hook by coming in and saying that Margaret had rung to say that there were more delays and we were to start without her. So there we were. Cosgrove emptied the ashtrays and took himself off, and I suggested we should make a move down-stairs to get stuck in to the buffet. As I opened the double door into the dining room, blow me if Boris, the new gardener, didn't pop up from behind some flower arrangement, playing out a length of flex to a wall-socket and explaining to me in that peculiar accent of his: "Zis dropical daffodil cannot sur-vive wizzout heat."

When I turned round, would you believe it, there was Heath tucking in his bib in M's chair at the head of the table. Anyway, I rang the bell and Cosgrove came in with the Avocado a la Prawns. Heath took one look at his and waved it away, saying: "Do you realise that the calorie content of one of those is the equivalent of two double whiskies?" This seemed a useful cue for me to go and refill my glass, and since M. wasn't there I saw no harm in bringing the bottle to the table. I was the recipient of another fishy glare from our sea-faring friend.

"These European Elections are the most crucial historical turning point since I took Britain in," Heath then announced. Well, Bill, I don't mind confessing I was pretty nonplussed as to what to reply to this. However, inspiration came, and I said I had once played at Le Touquet but couldn't make head or tail of the course being laid out in metres. Heath peered at me for several seconds, then said: "You really ought to meet Denis Thatcher. I gather he's a golf nut. Can't talk about anything else." Then, leaning forward confidentially, he added: "Between ourselves, I gather he likes his drink."

Before I could put my oar in on that one, in stomped Boris, who fiddled about with the daffodils and said would we mind speaking up. Pretty rum, eh Bill? But I've been told to keep a low profile by the Boss, so low profile it shall be. When Cosgrove brought in the cold pork and Russian Salad Heath took one look at it, gave a snort, and shouted: "She may not have much of a grasp of common courtesy but I bloody well have. Sod this for a lark, I'm going." As you can imagine, Bill, I was pretty relieved to see the back of the fellow and what's more when M. showed up two hours or so later she didn't seem too put out. I was very baffled by the piece in the *Telegraph* next morning headed "Mystery surrounds Heath/Thatcher Summit", but these newspaper johnnies are a closed book to me.

As I told the Major, June the Tenth it is. Stoke Poges come hell or high water. Dinner at the French Horn. My shout.

Yours aye!

DENIS

PS. By the way, you remember that delightful Mrs Datchet who used to live somewhere near Stoke Poges? Did she ever re-marry?

15 JUNE 1979

Dear Bill,

I hope this reaches you, as I gather the postal johnnies are playing silly buggers yet again.

By the way, whatever you do don't ring the home number again, at least for a bit! I gather the Major got an earful when he rang up on Budget Night. According to the Boss, any more calls after two a.m. and I'm for the high jump. From the sound of things the old boy was a bit plastered. (Was that you playing the piano in the background?) I tried to explain you only wanted to convey your congratulations on the Budget, but M. was absolutely livid and came all the way up to the boxroom in her slippers to read the Riot Act. Oh dear.

A propos the Budget, I was in a spot of hot water myself. I happened to be talking to some chaps in the RAC Club a couple of days before the Big Day, and Reggie Stebbings — very intelligent chap in insurance who's got his ear to the ground — said he wouldn't be half surprised if they didn't bump up the price of booze and he was thinking of popping down to Barrett's to lay in a goodly store.

Well, I asked Her Ladyship that evening if she thought there was any truth in it, and did she hit the roof! Official Secrets Act, Queen Juliana, contempt of Court, Muldergate, she threw the lot at me. In the end I wished I hadn't opened my mouth. A few minutes later in comes Howe from next door. I don't know whether you know him — some sort of lawyer by trade, harmless enough but a bit of a worrier, rather under his wife's thumb I always think. "Well, PM," he says, bouncing in through the door, "the boffins have worked it all out and I can't see why we shouldn't get away with it, at least for a few months." "Drink?" I suggested, trying to put him at ease and swinging open the cabinet. "Yes," says the little chap, "sixty p. on a bottle of Scotch."

At this point M. gave him one of her looks and took him off to the Holy of Holies, but I'd already twigged what was in the wind and bustled out to ring you lot and tip you the wink. As bad luck would have it, Boris was in the process of dismantling the telephone, so no joy. He told me it's his hobby, and apparently he's building his own "ham" transmitter out of old egg-boxes on the roof. Anyhow, down to the Liquormart in a jiffy, three crates in the boot — I reckon it was a saving of about ten quid — not to be sniffed at in these hard times, as the Major would say! Just backing into the only parking space available outside Number Ten when who do I collide with but old Howe standing on the pavement outside Number Eleven waving a tatty briefcase about, grinning like the proverbial Cheshire Cat and having his picture taken by the usual bunch of yobs with flash-bulbs.

Not my day as it turned out. No sooner had I started to unload than they turned round and snapped away at me. Front door opens, out pops the Boss. Lot of poppycock about tradesmen coming to the wrong address, going round the back, told to go to Number Nine, anyway I was to take it all back this minute, me left looking a damn fool. Not easy you know, Bill, all those bloody tourists looking on.

After all this, as you can imagine, I can't wait for Wednesday. Eastbourne it is. Lunch at the Grand and drinks on the way back with the Major's father at the Home.

T.T.F.N.

Yrs aye,

DENIS

---

10 Downing Street
Whitehall

29 JUNE 1979

Dear Bill,

Terribly sorry about Eastbourne. I should have looked in the book. As it was I got roped in for the Strasbourg show. Last thing I wanted to do, but M. put her foot down and ours not to reason why.

This Common Market stuff is all Greek to me. As you know, I'm not too hot on the local lingo, but luckily I ran into some chaps on a trade delegation from Edgbaston who'd absolutely given up, and while M. was doing her stuff with Giscard and Co. and that fat chap with glasses who used to be on the other side, we all sidled off to a very nice little snug at the Golden Goose, where they spoke decent English and all of us got faintly whistled. Everything on expenses, of course! Nothing but praise for the Boss, by the way. All these Birmingham blokes were cock-a-hoop about the Budget. Great plans for little residences in Majorca and places, and the Managing Director chap told me he thought he'd never have to work again. Lucky sod. (Talking of that. What about old Jeremy Thorpe getting away with it? Makes you think, doesn't it?)

To tell you the truth, I was rather looking forward to the Jap jaunt. Not first of all, because frankly that Carter chap gives me the heebie-jeebies. Fancy walking around in public holding hands with his wife at his age! Imagine me and M. getting up to that sort of lark! People would think I was a bloody lunatic. However, a week or so before we were to entrain I got a jolly nice invite from some Jap concern who make electric cars or something of that nature for three days of golf on their artificial Golferama place outside Kobe. Sticky Wilkinson played their five years ago and apparently it's out of this world. A bar at every hole, Geishas to carry your clubs, your balls bleep so you always know where they are, and the whole thing's under a gigantic sort of perspex dome with artificial sunlight so you can play all night. What price Littlestone, eh Bill?

I accepted like a shot I can tell you, and Cosgrove popped down to the Travel people to make arrangements. Not having a lot to do in the morning I thought I'd call in at Lillywhite's on the way to a pre-lunch snifter at the RAC and get myself a new Number Six Iron. I left my old one behind at Maidenhead that day Mrs Thingummybob passed out on the fairway. Anyway, got back a bit late for lunch, and oh dear, Proprietor displeased. The Major's postcard, very witty in its way, had rather backfired. I don't know whether you saw it, but it was a sort of seaside job, perfectly inoffensive in its way, and read: "Lucky old you. Tokyo Bound, eh? Reggie Stebbings recom-

13

mends Knocky Knocky Massage Parlour opp. Kishimoto Hotel. Number One Bang Bang".

Poor old Boris practically had to scrape me off the walls after Her Ladyship had finished with me, and I wouldn't be surprised if the Major's ears weren't burning a bit either.

Long and short of it, Yours Truly Not Wanted On Voyage.

Boris is turning out to be rather a nice chap by the way. Rough diamond of course — I imagine all the Russkies are. While M. was away I thought it an opportune moment to get the Rolls out of mothballs, and we tootled off to Wargrave with Boris at the wheel, self popping down in back seat

coming out of Downing Street, low profile and so forth, to avoid comment by Press yobboes outside front door. He told me fascinating things about Russia. Apparently there are 423 different kinds of Vodka. Did you know that?

See you on the 4th for the Inner Wheel do at Sevenoaks. Black tie, I presume.

Yours in the doghouse,

DENIS

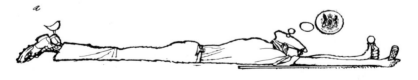

10 Downing Street
Whitehall

13 JULY 1979

Dear Bill,

Sorry about going AWOL on your Rotary. Usual thing, last-minute *froideur* from M. Of course I could go, but. . . Probably just as well in view of what transpired. I gather from the Major things got a bit out of hand and the bread rolls were flying. If I'd been there no doubt we'd have made the front page of the *Daily* bloody *Mirror*. Ah well, cakes and ale in very limited supply.

The Major told me you'd had a bit of a barney over those Boat People being let in. It must seem very rum from down there, and I don't want you to think I'd let the side down. On the contrary.

When the whole thing blew up in the first place M., as you know, put her foot down. Very right and proper. God knows the place is swarming with darkies of all 57 varieties as it is. I foam at the mouth on that topic as everyone in the Clubhouse will testify, especially when I've had a snort or two, and M. is basically in agreement, whatever she has to say in public. Strong support from K. Joseph.

Basically it was all Cosgrove's fault. Last Wednesday had been absolutely beastly: baking hot and all sorts of Union hobbledehoys tramping in and out with smelly socks, leaving a ghastly pong about the place. Proprietor displeased as you can well imagine; yours truly upstairs having completed *Telegraph* crossword puzzle except for three clues, tongue hanging out.

The plan was for Cosgrove to leave us a slap-up cold buffet with all the trimmings. M. had asked Stevarse round — not my favourite person in all the world — and I'd intended to take a plate upstairs with a noggin or two out of my cache in the attic and watch the International Golf on the box.

Alas. The moron Cosgrove had gone to a religious poetry reading. Cupboard bare. Stevarse mincing about putting the pictures straight and making damnfool jokes to cover up, but M. white at the gills. I suggested we all amble up to Wilton Street for a snack, but oh no. Stevarse on dangers of conspicuous extravagance. As bachelor he has far better scheme. Magic Number. A1 Chinese Takeaway delivered to Your Door. Orders Grand Feast for Three Persons: Sweet and Sour Lobster Tails, Crispy Balls, Peking Hot Crab — you know the form.

In the meantime, Carrington shimmers in his brothel creepers. Stevarse very miffed as the boss seems to have taken rather a shine to P.C.

(Peter Carrington turns out to be a very nice sort of chap, no side whatsoever, and he was at Eton with Sticky Wilkinson, so Sticky tells me, although Carrington didn't remember the name.)

Come nine-thirty, everyone a bit squiffy. Stevarse's jokes all falling very flat. Carrington getting no end of giggles from M. with impersonations of Q. Hogg etc. Suddenly serious note struck by Carrington. Boat People drowning like rats. Reminiscences of time Out East. Loyal little Ghurkas, Chindits etc. To tell the truth Bill, I began to feel a bit of a lump in the throat. Took me back, I don't mind telling you. Old days in Burma, etc. Carrington removed spectacles, wiped eyes.

At this juncture, bell rings and enter Chinese nosh-wallah with steaming cartons and obliging manner. Clearly no stranger to Stevarse, who tucks ten pound note in his top pocket and sends him on his way rejoicing. "There you are, Margaret," says our Norm. "Lot more where he came from. Very co-operative little people. Clean as a whistle. No local resentment. Try their hand at anything." M. seemed hesitant, but it suddenly struck me that it all made sense. Do you remember the last time we played at Deal? Couldn't get a caddy for love or money. Why not let these Boat Johnnies in and hey presto, caddy problem solved. Emboldened by the odd snort of Old Stag's Breath, and possibly just a touch blotto, I embarked on a harangue. Everyone spellbound. Haven't had a better reception since Reggie Stebbings's wife's funeral. Carrington misty-eyed. Stevarse arguing plausibly in favour of servant problem for returning tax-exiles, good gimmick etc. All turn to M. for response.

Chews on lobster leg for a bit, wipes chin, then says: "All right. How many?"

I must confess I stumped off up to Bedfordshire in something of a glow. Not often one has one's hand on the National Tiller, what? I think I may be cut out for this decision-making lark after all. M. filthy headache next morning, but no reversal of policy.

More soon. Yours till Hell freezes over,

DENIS

10 Downing Street
Whitehall

27 JULY 1979

Dear Bill,

What topping weather we've been having, and golly do I envy you the afternoon at Broadstairs! As you know, I tried to get away, only to be given a very severe wigging from the Boss about fuel conservation and an immediate directive to remove the personalised number plates from the Rolls. (My initials apparently open to misconstruction!!)

All in all, not a good week, Bill. I find a lot of the time hanging rather heavy on my hands. Westminster seems a particularly bad area for greenfly, and the roses in the garden were covered in the little blighters. Anyway, I took it into my

head to get the old stirrup pump out of the attic and give them a good drench with the new Fisons CHXO3. Blow me, no sooner had I got the bucket out — old Boris happy as a grig other end of the garden reading one of those foreign newspapers — than the window goes up and Her Ladyship is banging on about sodding things up with the Ministry of Environment — who does what — hard enough to get civil servants as it is etc. Ah me.

What I can't understand is that they seem to be massacring the Civil Servants like flies. I don't know whether you've seen that chappie Keith Joseph on the telly at all, but in my book he really is a bit of a four-letter fellow, and what's more, for our own private consumption, I'd be very surprised if they'd let him in at Hampstead Golf Club. Carrington, who I really have got to like awfully, calls him the Mad Monk, after that Svengali chap who put the kibosh on the Tsar. He's been in and out of the place like the proverbial dose of salts. Cut this, cut that, sell off the Post Office, railways back to Private Enterprise, North Sea Oil back to the Americans. Where will it all end, I ask you, Bill?

Mind you, they've obviously got to do something, the way things are going.

Emboldened by my intervention on behalf of the little yellow-skinned folk in the boats, I told them all as much the other night. M. had asked HQ staff back to the house for a bacon sandwich and a glass of port after the day's work — to celebrate old Thorneycroft's seventieth birthday — no sign of him packing it in, I regret to say — and the Mad Monk dropped by with a list of new cuts, including the Lifeboat Service, the Fire Brigade, and Museums. Stevarse and Carrington got very shirty about this, the former banging on in his usual arty-crafty mimsy manner about our bloody heritage. I ask you, Bill, who really gives a hoot about a lot of old Greek Jars and bits of bric-a-brac? I didn't say anything at this stage, but I could see Humpty Dumpty, i.e. Thorneycroft, getting a bit hot under the collar, and the situation began to look a bit ugly.

However. Somebody, it may have been Carrington, started in about all the dire consequences that would inevitably ensue from the Monk's cuts. Higher school meals, higher council house rents. "Look here," I said. Sudden hush. "I was talking to my friend the Major last night on the phone." They all looked a bit blank at this, so I seized the moment for another quick snort to oil the wheels. "Very nice chap," I explained. "Used to be in the RASC and then went into biscuits. Now he's flogging greenhouses in Tunbridge Wells." More blank looks. "He lives in a little village just outside Hastings. Do you know, there's a chap living in a council house in the Major's village — can't remember the name off-hand" — which I couldn't: Wittering? Twittering? Remind me. No matter. "Anyway, there's a chap living in a council house in this place who earns £400,000 a year, moonlighting with one thing and another, Daimler outside the door, kids at public school, obviously goes all over the world: now, I think this is the point, these council house buggers have obviously got jam on it. Motor-driven shower goes wrong in his bloody solarium — there's some wretched man from the council round in five minutes to fix it. If you seriously think a few quid on the rent is going to hurt these spongeing sods you must all be mad."

Harsh words, you may think, Bill, but honestly, the trouble with Carrington, charming drinking companion though he may be, is that his experience of the ordinary man in the street is precisely nil. To be fair to him, I think he took the point. Stevarse made funny faces and looked at the ceiling, but otherwise there was a feeling my words had gone home. I tottered off to bed then, but there was a good deal of laughter and merriment below for some time, and I got the impression that things are going our way.

By the by, I got talking to one of those Press johnnies who ring up from time to time trying to trip me up, and he told me that there's a marvellous clover-leaf course outside Barflor, or somewhere like that, in Normandy. You can get over quite easily on the Hovercraft — licensed all the way across — and it sounds just the thing for a thirsty lot like us: he said a double gin is fifteen pee and over on the other side it's all in francs. Bit of a change from the Old Mermaid. Would you have a word with the Major and see whether it might be feasible?

Yours in the pink,

DENIS

10 Downing Street
Whitehall

10 AUGUST 1979

Dear Bill,

Sorry I haven't been in touch before but I've been laid up with Lusaka Tummy ever since our return from the Dark Continent. God, what a trip! I must say I was jolly glad to set foot on British soil once more.

You know me, Bill, I've never had much time for our Dusky Cousins and this latest outing only went to confirm what everyone else calls my prejudice, but what you and I and the Major know full well is just plain common sense. To begin with it's bloody hot, Bill. 150° in the shade and there's precious little of that. After ten minutes in the hotel I was completely dehydrated and gasping for a long cool lotion, not to say two or even three. I rang for room service and this waiter johnny staggered in dressed up as a rear admiral, took a quid off me and I never saw the blighter again.

That's the sort of thing that happens in these parts.

Peter Carrington was the only one who had the right approach, I thought. You probably saw that the Nigerians had the bright idea of grabbing all of BP's assets. Can you imagine that, Bill? We go out there with all the kit, teach them how to burrow down and suck it up, and then the shifty little buggers turn round and seize it just as soon as our back's turned. Anyway, Carrington was at this reception along with me and the Boss, and he went up to their Ambassador or whatever and gave the fellow a good dressing-down.

When he'd finished, I came over and gave him a piece of *my* mind. M., however, intervened while I was in mid-stream and afterwards I was given a bit of a wigging and told to keep out of that sort of thing. But I still think I did right, Bill. You treat these buggers firmly and they respect you for it.

I gather a lot of people think the Boss has backed down a bit on this Rhodesia business. Fact of the matter is, Bill — but for Christ's sake keep it under your hat — that she had no choice. I can tell you this because of what happened on Day 2.

After breakfast (half a paw-paw and a pretty odd-looking sausage) I'm given my marching orders by M. Report 09.00 hours to the Royal Victoria Zambian Championship Links 10 miles out of town (get the old boy out of the way, what?). To be candid, Bill, I was glad to escape from the cocktail circuit and get a breath of fresh air on the golf course — or rather Hot Air, what?

You could have knocked me down with a feather when I discovered who my partner was — none other than HRH the D of E, no less, who as it turned out was in the same boat as yours truly, i.e. Not Wanted On Voyage, putting foot in it all over the shop and generally sticking out like a sore thumb at a wedding party. We got on like a house on fire from the start, Bill. I tell you, he's one of us, and a damn good egg who likes a snort as much as the next man.

You can tell why Zambia has so far failed to produce a Ben Hogan or an Arnold Palmer. The fairways have got about as much grass on them as Margate beach when the tide's out, and the so-called greens are made of lino. You hit a perfect pitch- shot, only to see a herd of wildebeeste or some such charging across in a cloud of dust and gobbling up the balls as if they were mushrooms.

After two holes, having lost all his Maxflies, the Duke turned to me and said: "Sod this for a lark, Thatcher. Where's the watering-hole?" (That's the way he talks.) He'd taken the words from my mouth, Bill, and in no time at all we were ensconced on the verandah of quite a decent club-house (run by a frightfully nice man from Carshalton who was in the Royal Artillery with Reggie Stebbings. Small world, eh Bill?)

Anyway, the Duke and I got chatting about this and that and the other and he let slip that he doesn't think too much of these Front Line Presidents or whatever they call themselves either. His solution for Rhodesia's the same as mine:

Re-organise the country.

Lift the sanctions.

Sod the lot of them.

The snag is this, Bill. HM, as he calls her, is in fact frightfully keen on all the Commonwealth shindig. Loves the whole palaver. White Goddess drops out of sky in great silver bird, crowds turn out, hordes of little piccaninnies waving Union Jacks, naked women dancing up and down shaking their whatsits — she laps it up, Bill, would you believe it? Kaunda, Nyerere, all of them, the bee's knees in her book. Won't hear a word against them. No choice for me but to tell M. what the form is. No more of this Carrington malarkey, kiss and make up with Kaunda and eat humble pie.

End result — all the nig-nogs beaming and smiling and singing ghastly songs, while M. and I put a brave face on it.

By the way, Bill. When HRH and I were having our chinwag at the nineteenth he passed on to me a little tin of ground rhinoceros horn. "Very tricky to get," he says, "with all these preservation orders about the place." Damn me if M. doesn't mistake the stuff for Coffee-Mate and puts it in the Gold Blend. Result: four days chained to the Mahogany! Absolute hell, Bill.

Should be back in circulation in a couple of days so I'll see you at Sandwich on the 18th. I've brought you back a little souvenir — a bottle of the local fire-water made out of fermented bamboo shoots — and it packs a powerful punch. Two snorts and you're out like a light.

Yours, aye,

DENIS

10 Downing Street
Whitehall

Dear Bill,

Oh dear. I realise I put up a terrible black vis a vis our Sandwich jaunt. The Major's telegram expressing his displeasure was fortunately misspelt by the Post Office otherwise I'd have been in hot water again with the Proprietor. What had gone clean out of my mind were M's holiday plans, which for some reason I had failed to pencil in my little book.

We got back from Scotland on the Flying Fornicator at seven o'clock this morning, and I'm still feeling pretty groggy. However much I hate this place, a week on the Isle of Muck or whatever it's called makes it seem like a positive Shangri-La.

I'm very confused about the whole thing, but it seems to have all been Macmillan's fault. He told the Boss that the done thing was a week in Scotland every August going after the grouse. Damn silly idea if you ask me, especially when all good men and true are out on the links at the Royal and Ancient.

I never caught the name of our host, but he had a handle to his name and used to be something very big in M's lot. He lives in the most ghastly God-forsaken castle on this frightful island covered with boulders and fir trees and not so much as a putting green in sight, somewhere out in the Celtic twilight you get to in a little aeroplane from Glasgow.

You know me, Bill. I can't tell a grouse from a bloody emu and I haven't fired a shot in anger since we went on that TA booze-up with the Major's mob at Deal. However, when I asked to be let off games, M. got unbelievably shirty. Down to the gun-room by the ear, kitted out in His Lordship's spare waterproofs and a damn silly hat with a lot of flies stuck in it, all several sizes too big. I ask you, Bill. Good thing none of the photographer johnnies were about otherwise I should have made the front page of *Gay News*, I can tell you. M's argument that it was no use being in a sulk, gratitude to our host and so forth: all I had to do was stand by the little flag and blast off a

couple of times to show willing.

What we had to be grateful for I really don't know. Everything they say about the Scots is absolutely true. Lord Whatsisname's idea of a snort looks as though a gnat's pissed in the bottom of the glass. Luckily, prior to the Shooting Expedition, I struck up a great friendship with the Factotum, who used to work for Royal Dutch, and he loaned me an awfully ingenious flask that fitted down the gumboot, filled with his favourite tipple, made at a secret still up in the hills somewhere. I meant to bring you back some, but unfortunately I got rather depressed on the train. Sorry about that.

Anyway, picture the scene. Rain bucketing down. His Lordship's reachmedowns leaking like the proverbial colander. M. got up in her best tweeds with a macintosh hat, deep in conversation with His Nibs. Yours Truly skulking in the butts under the watchful eye of one Ben Rubinstein, the local ghillie. Not one of the most talkative of souls, Bill: the odd grunt and a yellow-toothed snarl was about the sum of his repertoire.

After an eternity of waiting, barbaric cries from the undergrowth, a few bedraggled boiler fowl come winging in, barely visible in the mist. Auld Ben strikes me heavily between the shoulder blades and grunts something in Gaelic which I fail to catch, fowling-piece discharges into the butts, Auld Ben casts eyes heavenwards. Obviously no confidence in Bwana. Thoughts of D.T. at this juncture need not be described.

Scene Two. Another part of the forest. Same set-up: winds up to Force Nine, rain now horizontal, specs entirely steamed up, Wellingtons filling nicely. A few sheep cropping the rocks. Lord Thingummybob plainly in his element, talking to M. about the old days with Winston. At that point, Bill, something snapped. No one watching, so I gave old Snaggleteeth five quid and the gun, and buggered off back to the castle.

Hot bath, dry togs, large noggin of firewater, and settled down in Back Nursery to watch International Golf. Much to my relief my absence did not appear to have registered with the Big White Chief, or indeed Mine Host. Ghastly dinner of boiled birds, all bones and buckshot, no fizz in sight. Sympathetic shrugs from kilted majordomo, but the message is No Can Do. Meanwhile Lord Whatsisname is telling M.

how much he approves of axeing the students, far too many long-haired clever dicks about the place as it is. High time student grants were cut out altogether and they were all turned over to potato picking. (Not a bad wheeze when you think of it, Bill. Half the cheek you and I have encountered over the past few years has come from that sort of person.)

By the way, Bill, trust old Heath to emerge from the Fastnet show with not a hair out of place. I said as much to M. while we were looking for our bedrooms the other night, and got my ear bitten off as you might expect. In her book, there's no doubt about it, Heath is definitely Right Marker of the Shits' Brigade, but in politics you don't go round saying that sort of thing. So for Christ's sake don't go quoting me in the Snug.

Reggie says there's rather a nice little indoor driving range near London Airport. Would that be a possible venue to bob back a few scoops?

Yours, through a glass darkly,

DENIS

---

10 Downing Street
Whitehall

14 SEPTEMBER 1979

Dear Bill,

Well, Bill, we live in stirring times, no doubt of that. This Mountbatten business has been pretty sickening all round: apart from anything else I'll have to scratch the outing to Hunterscombe. Peter Carrington told me that from now on if I go anywhere out of doors I have to have some Special Branch man in a dirty mac traipsing about in my wake, shaking the clubs out every time I want to play a shot, and peering through the window, no doubt, at the Nineteenth to avert foul play. I told Carrington that quite honestly I'd rather stay at home watching the telly than go along with all that sort of caper. But things have come to a pretty pass, Bill, when a chap

27

can't even take the clubs for a walk because some thick-headed Irish hooligans want to play silly buggers.

The funny thing is, the Boss seems to be having a bit of a ball over the whole thing. No sooner had the balloon gone up than our enterprising Italian friends from Saatchi's were round with the kit, full camouflage flak jacket and khaki bloomers with a sort of brown tam o'shanter and a six-gun, for a whistle-stop tour of the black spots. The name of the game, obviously, was showing the flag. Frankly I couldn't see the sense in it but I was absolutely prepared to go along to provide moral support if necessary, doing my D of E bit, tagging along, hands clasped behind the back. However, suggestion sat on very firmly by Chairperson. Ours not to reason why, eh Bill?, so I was grateful for a few hours' peace.

I found old Boris rootling about in M's drawers looking for some file or other, so I invited him into the Pantry upstairs where I normally take the portable, and we watched a bit of the Test Match with a bottle of his mother's sloe vodka. Awfully nice chap. One of nature's gents. I've never understood why we can't get on with the Russians. But M. as you know doesn't see eye to eye with me on that one.

On the other hand, I was able to get a word in edgeways on the bloody bogtrotters. The scheme devised by Peter C. was that Lynch, the little bald chap who works as the Trossack or whatever they call M's equivalent in the Land of the Leprechauns (and incidentally, what a dump it is: do you remember the time the Major rented that ghastly bungalow in Galway and it pissed with rain every day for two weeks? No wonder they're all half cut ninety per cent of the time — I know we were). Anyway, Lynch is a shifty little fellow in suede brothelcreepers and a Meakers off-the-peg jacket who looks like a bookie — very like that chap who used to run the bar at Deal and went AWOL with the funds. I spotted his form a mile off. Made a beeline for the drinks tray and if I hadn't been there a split-second before him my guess is he'd have polished off three inches of my Glen Morangie which I was reserving for the social rigours.

Anyway, as I say, the plan was to have him in after the Westminster Abbey do and rub his nose in it. I told M. beforehand while we were getting into our Moss Bros. funeral weeds that she was wasting her time with our Irish friends, and sure enough, after an hour of talks, with Carrington and the Boss pinning him to the desk and bellowing at him, result precisely nil. Usual stock waffle handed out to the Presswallahs. Lynch came out first, looking bloody devious, and having got fairly stoked up in the interim I felt I had to give him a piece of my mind. I told him about the Galway trip and the Major falling in the river and pointed out that we didn't need to go there in the first place, and that that went for the whole shebang. They've been bloody lucky to have us for however many hundred years it is we've been pumping money into their off-shore peatbog, and if I had my way we should just pull the plug out and let them fight it out among themselves like the pack of rats they are.

My God, Bill, it sent his eyebrows up a good way. No doubt at all, that's the kind of language they understand. Needless to say, M. bore down on me like an ice-breaker. I was crushed against the wall and consigned to outer darkness. Usual guff about hot pursuit — M. determined to get on top of the gunmen, Carrington banging on about not giving in to the men of violence, and if we all pull out there'll be a bloodbath.

Well, what the hell does he think is going on at the moment? That's what I'd like to know, Bill.

I was jolly miffed about the whole thing, I don't mind telling you, especially when Lynch tugged his forelock on the doorstep and said could he have three million for a cup of tea or something. But it's no use talking to these politicos, Bill, that's what I've discovered. The whole thing's as plain as a pikestaff to you or me, but they can't see it.

How long I am to be in Purdah I have no idea: we've got this Rhodesian nonsense all this week. I think I can manage lunch at the Club if you're going to be in Town at all. My Special Branch Shadow is called Eric and comes from Haywards Heath. Quite a nice chap but strictly TT. Some kind of Methodist I think. Probably persuade him to have lunch in the Rabbit Food place across the way from the Members' Entrance.

My best to Daphne. Glad she enjoyed her trip to the Bahamas.

Yours,

DENIS

---

10 Downing Street
Whitehall

28 SEPTEMBER 1979

Dear Bill,

It seems donkeys' years since we had a proper pow-wow and a few snorts. To be perfectly frank I'm beginning to feel like the Man in the Iron Mask locked up in this confounded talking shop. For your ears only, Eric my bodyguard is the most bloody

awful drip I have ever encountered. His latest wheeze is to try and get me onto the water wagon. It's got to the stage where I can't open the drinks cabinet without him giving me a beady look and going "Tut tut tut!". Bloody fool. I told him frankly Bill that I wasn't going to stand for it: by the time you get to our age either you can take it or you can't.

Can you imagine it, Bill? Every time I go down to the Club for elevenses this flatfoot comes plodding along behind me with his socks hanging down, looking exactly like that flasher who used to hang about near the fifteenth at the Royal and Ancient and who gave Daphne such a nasty turn that time you and I got unavoidably detained.

I've been trying to keep my head below the parapet this week anyway during the Rhodesian Gathering. But it's been real murder. Every night I've had to get done up in my Mess kit for one or other of the Paramount Chiefs. Needless to say, the festivities have not gone by without the odd clanger being dropped by yours truly. For one thing they all look exactly the same to me except for the fat one, and for the life of me I can't understand a word any of them says.

On Wednesday for example we all had to go to Buck House for a stand-up scoff in one of the larger rooms at the back. As bad luck would have it, I got stuck with a little sky-pilot chap in glasses whose name I didn't catch, and who seemed nice enough in his way. Low Church, and spoke very well of the missionaries. I asked him if he ever played golf and he didn't seem to catch on, so after a while I tried again. "What do you think of this Prime Minister bloke you've got over there — Ian Smith?" (Bit of an H.M.G. [Home Made Gent] in my opinion but I obviously didn't say as much.) Next thing I know I'm left holding our black friend's plate of chicken curry and he's out the door like a streak of greased lightning. Scene Two, a few moments later — self propping up mantelpiece with D of E discussing life under the iron heel, up pops Peter Carrington, accoutrements askew, exceedingly fussed. Do I realise I have ruined entire conference by insulting the Prime Minister? It turns out, you see Bill, that the chap I was talking to was none other than Bishop Whatsit, who was now very miffed and downstairs in the yard talking about flying the whole delegation back to Nyasaland. I refrained from saying that it might be a jolly good thing if they all buggered off for the duration, and had to go downstairs cap in hand and plead temporary insanity due to war wound playing up. But I said to Peter Carrington afterwards that they really ought to get themselves sorted out. After all, how was I to know it was the PM? Bishops are one thing, and Prime Ministers are another. You and I would have thought it pretty odd in the old days to have a padre on the Burmah Board, let alone running the whole bang-shoot.

(Incidentally, Bill, between ourselves, did you know that one of M's jobs was appointing the Archbishop of Canterbury? I took the liberty of putting forward old Archie Wellbeloved now that he's retired: I know he often gives the impression he's not all there, but he's pretty good through the green and preaches a very nice little sermon, as you and I discovered at the Wilkinson funeral: all in the Saloon Bar by twelve on the dot, as I recall. However, I was told that I was talking out of turn again, that everything had been fixed and this goof from St Albans with the talkative wife had it in the bag all along.)

Anyway, the whole African Circus has struck camp now and sodded off. The Captains and the Kings depart, eerie silence falls etc. etc. and the Boss seems to have patched up some sort of deal about sanctions. But quite honestly Bill, what difference will it make with a full-scale Zulu war raging to and fro and the British box-wallahs getting the hell out of it as fast as their sun-bronzed knees can carry them? I was saying to Boris only the other day, while I was helping him fix his new television aerial on the roof, it beats me why we have to get mixed up in that sort of caper when we're in it up to here as it is with British Leyland and so on. He made the point I might have a word with M. along those lines, but he's a bachelor of course and doesn't understand the form.

Talking of that, if Daphne's off again on her travels, why don't you and I have a little stag outing on one of those Thomson's Winterbreaks? You have to be at Luton at five o'clock in the morning, but I gather the booze flows as per normal once you're aloft. They tell me they have a very good offer of three days in Corfu all in for £92.50, where, as you know from the Major's reminiscences, they have that extraordinary course with ponds instead of bunkers. According to my informant, a Greek chap I ran into at the Club, the place is swarming with frogs, who set up their caterwauling whenever a ball lands anywhere near.

Yours in high dungeon,

DENIS

Dear Bill,

Too soon, too soon! It seems I was somewhat premature in my last screed re the Rhodesian shindig. Boris, who is the only one who ever knows what's going on, tells me they haven't gone after all, and Peter Carrington is still shimmering to and fro from one Kensington bordello to another trying to patch things up. I've told him he's wasting his time, but once these chaps have got their noses into it there's no earthly use trying to whistle them off.

Our little friend Cosgrove was in hot water last week, I'm glad to say. I don't know whether you have been watching this spy story on the goggle-box — it's called *Tinker Tailor Soldier Sailor* and it's all about these hush-hush Intelligence johnnies and how they make a hash of everything. I haven't been able to make head or tail of it. Boris, on the other hand, has been absolutely glued. So, for that, matter, has the Boss.

For your ears only, this is how events unfolded. M., positively riveted to screen, can't take her eyes off Alec Guinness (who you may remember, Bill, we saw in the gloriously funny film in Deal many moons ago, *The Lavender Killers*). Cosgrove shaking nuts into various saucers in background, generally being pretty sniffy about it. No sooner is it over than he chirps up: "Of course, Ma'am, it's not really a bit like that in the real Secret Service." Proprietor highly displeased. I thought it prudent to withdraw to drinks cupboard, but overheard ensuing dialogue while measuring self a stiff sherbet.

Boss: "I happen to know on the highest authority that the main character, Smiley, is based on my old friend Sir Maurice Oldfield, the head of MI6, now retired, and how many times do I have to tell you to wipe those ashtrays out with a damp cloth?"

Cosgrove: "Very well, Ma'am. Was there anything else, or

35

can I go to bed?"

Boss: "Yes. Now you have brought it up, look up Sir Maurice's number in the telephone book. I think Sir Alec, I mean Sir Maurice, is just the man I need to be my top trouble-shooter behind the scenes in Northern Ireland."

You won't believe it, Bill, but that's the way things get done. The joke was, of course, that M. intended it all to be Boardroom Only, Highly Confidential stuff, whereas little know-all Cosgrove took it into his head to announce the whole bang shoot to the Press johnnies, thus ensuring that some blasphemous bogtrotter, regardless of the Pope's very sensible remarks, will blow the poor bugger sky-high on the basis of the snap published on the front page of the *Telegraph*.

I know you always thought Burmah in my time was an utter shambles, but I assure you, Bill, we had nothing on this lot.

However, miserable as I am at not being able to get away more often, I do sometimes feel I am able to bring a little sanity to bear. Do you remember that chap Maurice Picarda who used to run a couple of garages near Sevenoaks? Rough diamond, especially after a tincture or two — you probably recall the embarrassing evening at The Feathers with Polly Mountjoy, and whatever happened to her, by the way? — but he could putt like a demon and I've always had rather a soft spot for the old boy, not to say his missus, who is a sweetie. Anyway, he wrote me a frightfully decent letter the other day. His point was this. Were we Conservatives or weren't we? If we were, what the hell was Geoffrey Howe doing farting about with Company Perks, i.e. free cars? The tone of the letter, I confess, was very emotional, and he ended up by calling us a bunch of half-crazed sods.

Funnily enough, Howe happened to call by just before lunch and, emboldened by the pre-prandial lotion, I broached the topic, adding a point of my own, to wit who on earth could afford to buy these British Leyland limos at ten grand a time, and if it wasn't for the company perks the whole shooting match would go bust.

Odd chap Howe. Some kind of lawyer. Nothing against lawyers myself. Do you remember that solicitor in Fairlight who got done for fiddling the bar accounts? Awfully amusing chap, used to write to me from prison. Howe, anyway, seemed to take my point, and I was encouraged to go on and outline to him our old strategy at Burmah when every member of the Board automatically got a Rover. In the Major's firm, you remember, wives and children were similarly provided for. I also made him laugh no end with my old story about Sticky's trick with the cheque-stubs.

The long and the short of it is, Bill, that when he finally went off to the trough with M. — she was a bit late — Howe was absolutely roaring to do a U-turn on the whole thing. Sure enough, come closing time, Boss a new woman. No more nonsense of that sort. I rang Picarda to tell him the glad tidings. He sounded absolutely chuffed to naafibreaks, and has promised me a free limo on the strength of it. How about that, eh Bill? Who says Conservative Government isn't working?

Next week I'm afraid is a washout. Bloody bloody Blackpool. On parade every day, I imagine, so you can count me out vis a vis the nine holes you proposed at Wimbledon. Am I dreading it, Bill! Out every night, trailing along in the perfumed wake, pressing the flesh, grin grin, Young Conservative Pressure Group For Change from Penge, Wine and Cheese at the Top Rank Bingo Hall (no wine, precious little cheese), Stevarse traipsing about like a Piccadilly Penguin with an orange up its arse. I'll let you know, Bill, I'll let you know.

Meanwhile, spare a thought for your erstwhile chum in the snug,

DENIS

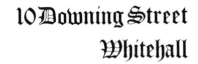

Dear Bill,

I hope you got the p.c. from Blackpool and Daphne wasn't too shocked — or is she not back yet from Bermuda? I've always liked that joke and I thought the drawing of the surgeon had a look of the Major about it.

The whole shemozzle ran pretty true to form, as you may have appreciated from what they showed on the telly. The tricky part as far as yours truly was concerned was staying awake during the long stretches after lunch. I was under a seven line whip from the Boss on that topic: my orders were to sit up under the lights in full view of the cameras and "try to look compos mentis", laugh at the right places and so-called "jokes", and clap at the appropriate moments. No easy brief, Bill, as you will appreciate, especially after taking a few tinctures at lunchtime.

Incidentally, I fell in with a most amusing little fellow called Palmer who claimed to have served under the Major at Caterham, and said he was never a major at all, but actually RSM in charge of stores! What about that, eh Bill? Next time I see the old boy I shall certainly rib him about it. Any rate, Palmer and I got on like a house on fire and found a charming little antiquey sort of snug just off the front where you could get Glen Morangie and not have to rub shoulders with creeps like Stevarse and Heseltine. Honestly, Bill, what a couple of four-letter fellows. I can't think why the Boss brings in that class of person. By God, have you got to watch them in the rough!

One person I have taken a terrific shine to is old Willie Whitelaw. A real gent of the old school, and what's more with a very decent handicap. Like me, the poor old buffer is much afflicted with the Special Branch. His is called Muffler and is, if anything, more grotesque in appearance than my frightful

Eric. He has already spoiled more than one potentially excellent afternoon by lurking about outside the Clubhouse improperly accoutred. We've hatched a plan to give them both the slip one day and pop down to Worplesdon for a few holes (inter nos).

Whitelaw I thought made the only good speech in the whole ballsaching business, saying what he was going to do to the hooligans, i.e. give them a short sharp taste of their own medicine and put a stop to all this namby-pamby do-gooder type of caper recommended by our friends on the *Guardian*. Incidentally, what about Princess Margaret calling the Irish pigs, eh? Glad to see I'm not the only one to put my foot in it over the bog-trotters. Absolutely right, of course: pigs is what they are, and always have been, and if one can't say what one thinks after a cocktail or two what's the point in being alive? As per usual these Press people were lurking behind every bush waiting to pounce. Buggers. I had half a mind to scribble a note to HRH expressing solidarity, but M. squashed it, needless to say.

What else is new, you ask? Well, everybody's getting very steamed up about the Common Market, as is only right and proper. M. knows my views on the subject, i.e. that we should never have got mixed up with the bally thing in the first place. It was obvious from the start that the Frog in the street wasn't going to jump at our stuff, give or take the odd woolly from Marks and Sparks, and they can always come over on the boat-train if they want one of those. So what's the point? Personally I blame that damn fool Heath. I've always said he was about as much use as a one-legged man at an arse-kicking party, and this lamb stuff is exactly what one would have expected.

I managed to bend Peter Walker's ear on the subject at Blackpool — another HMG by the way, but hats off to him for getting out of the City at the right time, unlike his little friend Slater — and I think he's on our side. I always remember that absurd hoo-ha about green fees at Bad Godesburg in '48. I realised then that this European Unity lark was a non-starter. Sticky, as you may remember, was in hospital for several weeks afterwards and had to go and be dried out at Spa, much to the Boche Club Secretary's amusement. M. however clearly got carried away with the Winston Churchill aspect of it all. I think I've told you she's never forgiven me for stubbing a cigarette out on a little china figurine of him she has on her dressing-table.

Odd the way the news came through about old Breshneff trickling down the sink. I'm surprised he's lasted as long as he has if Boris's Vodka's anything to go by. Constitution like an ox, though, according to the latter, and he's the only one here who's got his ear to the ground.

Did you get a circular from Whiffy about a Burmah Piss-Artists' Reunion at the Savoy? I thought it might be very agreeable if I can get someone to babysit with Eric: still trying to persuade me to sign the pledge, producing awful literature showing the havoc wrought by the demon alcohol. I think one of the snaps is of old Heatherington who used to be a regular at The Feathers.

Yours in spirit,

DENIS

Dear Bill,

Well well. Where will it all end? If you'd told me in '45 when you and I were in khaki and the Huns were flogging their wives and daughters for a packet of Woodbine Willies that we would end up grovelling about cap in hand trying to ingratiate ourselves I'd have said you were a raving bloody lunatic. It makes me so angry, Bill, I've had to go back on my blood pressure pills. Eric sniggering up his sleeve saying what do I expect, body will only stand so much ill-treatment. God rot the lot of them is what I say.

I gave the Boss a hint of my feelings when she first announced her intention of flying over to the Ruhr to try and win over Herr Schidt to our way of thinking on the Market. I was halfway through the *Telegraph* crossword puzzle at the time and I saw red. "If there's to be any truck with the Boche," I said, "let them come to us. If it wasn't for the fact that Harris and his lot did such a successful demolition job on Hamburg, Dresden and points North the buggers would never have got off the ground." Did old Fruity Purvis make the supreme sacrifice for this?, I asked her. It turned out of course that she didn't remember Fruity, but I have a perfectly clear recollection of her sitting next to him at Sticky's wedding. Were you there? Too long ago to recall, alas, but I would swear she was the only sober member present on that occasion.

Anyway, to cut a long story short, proprietor had her own way as usual, though she did agree to take a firm line with Jerry when she got there. It so happened that I was watching the news with Boris, waiting for the Golf to begin, and what do you think, Bill? Schidt standing there at the Press Conference wearing some nancy-boy U-boat hat, bloody well taking snuff off the back of his hairy German paw and trumpeting into his hanky like a rogue elephant all the time M. was trying to woo the media with soothing words. Even Boris got damn hot under the collar at that, Bill, I don't mind telling you. As you probably remember, they had a pretty rough time under the Hun and the spectacle clearly disgusted him to the point of opening a bottle of Hungarian vodka newly arrived in the diplomatic bag. (Did you know by the way that it's completely safe to drink that stuff? No effect on the liver whatsoever. Contains no impurities. Boris told me that, and I absolutely believe him. He often drinks two bottles on the trot without batting an eyelid.)

I'm beginning to think that Boris is really the only sound man we have in our little Colditz set-up here in Downing Street. The other thing he took an extraordinarily dim view of was the arrival of the Yellow Peril last week. Boss and Carrington rolling about like puppies waiting to have their tummies tickled by Mr Hu Flung Dung. Yours truly was wheeled out, despite protests, for the Muster Parade. That thing they say about not being able to tell them apart is absolutely true, you know. Hordes of little men poured into the Talking Shop. Fingers crushed to jelly, cramp in jaw muscles from grinning, just about to take refuge in the back pantry with the tincture bottle when Stevarse throws arm round shoulders, cuddles up close and tells me we're off to the Ballet at Covent Garden.

Bang goes my evening with the Celebrity Golf. Boris suggested I should take a portable into the back of the box — he knows all about that sort of thing because they have it in Russia — but I decided reluctantly that M. was in no mood to be trifled with, especially after that speech of Chairman Hu which caused great amusement among those Chinese speakers present and came out in translation as something to do with her wanting to wear Winston's trousers. However, Boris did fit me up with something in a flask to deaden the pain during the long hours of culture that lay ahead.

We got into our box all right, and I managed to bag a seat at the back where it was quite dark, behind a fat chap with bushy eyebrows who seemed to know all about it. After ten minutes of standing up and sitting down, just like that bit in the Marx Brothers film, the orchestra struck up and the curtain rose. Whereupon two dozen or so Bertie Wooftahs came prancing on pretending to be flowers. Bloody fools. I think I must have dozed off at that point. The next thing I knew, the fat man was nudging me and saying my snores were disturbing the dancers. I watched Hu for a bit after that, and I came to the conclusion that these Chinese chaps can sleep with their eyes open. No wonder they did so well against the Chindits. Apropos, frightfully sad about old Templar turning his toes up.

Stevarse, needless to say, flooded out in the interval into the little dining room they have at the back; in raptures about the whole shebang, fluttering around Hu like the proverbial moth. Wasn't he entranced by the Palais Glide and so forth, and throwing in a lot of French expressions that took a bit of fielding by the interpreter. I may say I succeeded in spending Acts II, III and IV in a nice little fizz-shop up in the Gods with a very cheery old body called Mrs Bloomer, who said they might all look very cultivated but you should see the mess after they've gone: cigar butts, rubber johnnies, everything apparently. At the end of it all I squeezed back behind Fatty in time to catch the Finale, which consisted of the same bunch of pansies dressed up as horny-handed sons of toil doing ring a ring o'roses round the village well.

I asked Stevarse afterwards if there was any chance of pulling the whole place down as part of Margaret's cuts, but he got frightfully sniffy and said it would be over his dead body.

Which is OK in my book, but I didn't say that.
See you on the 12th at Squiffy's. Promise no shop.
Yours,

DENIS

---

10 Downing Street
Whitehall

23 NOVEMBER 1979

Dear Bill,

Sorry about M's tetchiness when you phoned on Wednesday night, but things have been somewhat hectic of late and we've been a bit bogged down in the rough. Any little thing sets the old alarm bells going, and your query about why no more tax cuts after the Guildhall shindig on the telly clearly caught M. on the wrong foot. I should have warned you, I suppose, because I got a nasty nip in the seat of the pants only the day before.

As you know, Bill, economics have never exactly been my best shot, but this MLR caper is really too rum for words. I don't know whether I've mentioned it, but I have a very accommodating little bank manager I've discovered at my local NatWest round the corner in Victoria. Name of Furniss and keeps a very decent sherry in the safe. Nor is he averse, I may say, to one or two during working hours, which makes for a most relaxing relationship, I think you'll agree. Anyway, I popped in to pass the time of day on the way to lunch with Sticky at Simpson's, and the conversation eventually came round to my account, which just between the two of us is looking quite healthy at present, thanks to one thing and another.

Why not, says our banking friend, taking a sip of the amber tincture, slosh a bit of the current over into the deposit? "As from today", he says, pulling out a sheaf of publicity bumf from head office, "we're giving you a nice fat thirteen

45

and a half per cent before tax, and that can't be bad in anyone's language." Well, Bill, I thought that sounded a very sensible wheeze. Virtually no expenses nowadays, as many five-course dinners as you can eat, crates of the stuff appearing from well-wishers, not to mention the odd cadeau from tradesmen, and all the rest on HMG. I was always brought up to believe in the piggy bank. "Put something away for a rainy day," was what Uncle Jonah used to say: damn shame he never lived to spend it. (Liver, as you may remember, ran up the white flag. But cheerful to the last.) Put the money where it can do something. Very roughly, on the back of an envelope, I reckoned by next year I should be able to bung on a good six noughts, always assuming my mental arithmetic was accurate.

Be that as it may, inflation's no bloody joke — witness poor old Maurice Picarda having the receiver in at Tonbridge and forced to bring forward his holiday plans somewhat sharpish. Now you won't believe this, Bill, but when I got back to the shop I found Howe *a deux* with the Boss, having what I took to be a bit of a barney. When I had helped myself to a generous lotion to keep me going till they opened, I strolled in to see if I could offer any assistance. Although he's very quiet about it, I think Geoffrey Howe values my advice: voice from the grass roots and so forth, ear to the shop floor. I make my entrance. Comes a pause. Both looking a bit down in the mouth. "Well," says I, "I think things are going our way at last." "Oh," says M., "and why do you think that?" So, as you can imagine, Bill, I spooled out the yarn about my little chat with Friend Furniss and the thirteen and a half per cent business, thinking in all innocence that that was the name of the game.

Would you believe it, Bill, the Boss absolutely hit the ceiling. Howe all white and trembly, spectacles steaming on the nose, looking at me as much as to say, "Why couldn't you keep your bloody trap shut?", and me giving him my "How was I to know?" look. Turns out the last thing they want to know about is lending rates. M. absolutely Gale Force Eight, next thing we know the mortgages will be going up. Very foolish, looking back, but I put forward the argument that this might be no bad thing, instancing the Major doing so well with his own show, the Tonbridge Reliable. (Weren't you on the Board of that for a while? I think I was.) My God, did the solids hit the fan! I was treated to a sixteen and a half minute lecture on money supply, MLR, some boffin called Friedmann, all of which didn't make any sense to me, and a similar diatribe harping on my various shortcomings, which were all too painfully familiar. Howe didn't exactly come rushing to my support, I must say. But I realised he'd been having his ear pretty effectively chewed off before I blundered in.

Did I tell you I'm beginning to have my doubts about Peter Carrington? I rather think he may have done the dirty on us over the Rhodesia show. I had my suspicions about the Padre chap, Mazaratti or whatever he calls himself, but my hunch is that Carrington has patched up some sort of deal behind our backs with the fat one. I can't see what he hopes to get out of it, that's what puzzles me. But ah me, such is life.

Any chance of Daphne being back at Christmas? I thought we might try and fit in a few rounds at Lamberhurst over the Festive Tide, but the Boss may want to go to Chequers. Not my C of T at all. Full of draughty corridors, portraits of Disraeli, very antique shoppy. Boris I know is dreading it.

My best to Daphne if you're ringing the Bahamas.

TTFN,

DENIS

---

 10 Downing Street
Whitehall
7 DECEMBER 1979

Dear Bill,

I don't know what to say about what happened to the Major. I was up in my little snug in the attic at the time, having a jar with Boris, and all I heard was a bit of a melee taking place outside on the pavement, voices raised, glass breaking etc, which I put down to some left-wing weirdo or other making some protest or other, there always being a fair quota of that variety of customer hanging about outside the premises.

Putting the story together afterwards from what Eric my ghastly bodyguard told me, I came to the conclusion that the old boy had come up to town to do his Christmas shopping at Lillywhite's, and after a fairly liquid lunch at the Club had taken it into his head to call in for a tincture before setting off to Charing Cross. Alas, it appears that the Constable on the door mistook his peaceable intentions, bringing out the old Burmah spirit with a vengeance, and a bit of a fracas ensued, during which the Major stole the policeman's helmet and broke one of the downstairs windows. I rang up the Cop Shop, and managed to straighten things out with the chap on the desk after a bit of initial misunderstanding. The promise of a generous donation to the Christmas Ball and my offer to buy up the entire next issue of *Police News* seemed to assuage the wrath of the Boys in Blue, but I fear the incident still rankles with the Major. Do give the old boy my love and tell him there'll be something in his Christmas stocking.

I say, I think the Boss did the right thing vis a vis that swine Blunt, don't you? Did you see him on the TV by any chance? Crikey, what a roarer. I don't know how he ever passed his medical for the Palace. When the whole thing blew up I told the Boss not to go into bat on that one. Exceedingly sticky wicket. Have no qualms, said I, about dropping him right in it. And I've certainly been proved right.

The whole business struck me as very rum. Wilson pops up and says he knew about it all along, shifty little stoat. (I always thought the Sergeants' Mess didn't go along with that sort of thing!) And then it all comes as a complete surprise to old Home. As you know, Bill, I've always taken the line that Home was a gent, and gents told the truth. And yet, do you know, watching him on the box I could have sworn the old fraud was lying in his teeth. Anyway, it all appears to have been mopped up now, and I wasn't in the mood to raise it with the Proprietor, as her nerves haven't been all they might have been of late and the balloon is likely to go up at the slightest provocation.

The thing is, Bill, I'm not absolutely certain where we are. M. did her table-thumping number at the Common Market get-together in Dublin as you saw, without, it seems, anything very clear emerging, at least not from where I'm sitting. I had been hoping for a bit of a beano beside the Liffey, particularly after that glorious three days — or was it a week? — with you and Daphne the time we ran into the Major's mother in the Shelbourne when she fell over at four o'clock in the afternoon and had to be laid out on the tea-trolley, but anyway, F.O. said no can do, danger to life and limb, too much of a burden on security forces, so I popped down to Lamberhurst in the old Rolls and watched events wrapped around a bottle of Old Grandad. But not before being stuck for the best part of half an hour in one of the downstairs offices with that frightful HMG Roy Jenkins, who apparently runs the whole Common Market racket at their end and had come round to put the Boss in the picture. Talk about dropping names, Bill! We were ankle-deep in them, e.g. did I know any of the French Rothschilds? I said the only Rothschild I ever knew was that awfully decent little pawnbroker in Sandwich where you got that simulated mink for Daphne after the Rotary Dinner went wrong.

As I was saying, I can't help feeling a bit mystified by it all. Howe has a frightful haunted mien, and Joseph looks to me as though he was ripe for the Bin. As Picarda quite rightly complained in a lengthy reverse-charge call from Malta, all this talk about cutting taxes for our people seems to have gone for a burton, and now the teenage boffins in M's think-tank are talking about putting them up again! One hesitates to talk about the old girl being blown off course, but that's the way it's beginning to look. They keep going on about cutting the money supply, but I've never really understood how that was supposed to be achieved, unless of course you go round with collecting bags, as with saucepans during the war, gathering the surplus fivers all together in a heap and setting fire to the lot. I made this point to Howe the other day when he was hanging about in the hall, and he went very quiet. It made me wonder whether he understood it at all.

By the way, Bill, the Festive Tide being almost upon us, could you wangle us a crate or two of the Club port for distribution amongst my intimate circle? Just pop in the usual card and sign them for me if you would be so kind. I simply can't bear the thought of traipsing round Harrods with Eric in tow in his flat hat, not to mention the smell of all those Arabs. Good will to all men, I agree, but there are limits. Quite honestly I am beginning to dread the whole grisly business. Mark is threatening to descend with one of his hideous harem, and him and M. together, as you know, is oil and water. Must go now, Boris is leading me astray with a new consignment of Mother Russia's ruin.

Hope this finds you in the pink,
Your old chum,

DENIS

---

10 Downing Street
Whitehall

21 DECEMBER 1979

Dear Bill,

Oh God! I expect you saw that I made page two of the *Telegraph*. Not exactly calculated to ease my lot with the Boss over Yule. Talk about shits of hell: Fleet Street takes the biscuit. God knows I'm let off the leash seldom enough as it is, sitting in Downing Street all day long being told to lift my feet up every time little Cosgrove comes by with the hoover, and now this comes up.

What happened, Bill, was as follows: as you probably know, I've been toddling along to the Savoy for donkeys' years for some little do that Squiffy gets together in aid of Mentally Handicapped Referees or something of that nature, and I've never thought a thing about it. Quite a decent set of chaps, a few snorts, odd familiar face, all very agreeable. This year, it so happened, thanks to M's elevated status, one of the organisers who I think runs a garden centre just outside Maidstone said would I mind getting up on my hind legs and saying a word or two after the loyal toast. Anything on a sporting theme, absolutely off the record, press wallahs excluded and so on and so forth. I should have seen his form a mile off: a real greaser of the old school and HMG to boot.

Anyway the time trickled by, and come the great day mind still a perfect blank. Boris gave me quite an amusing story about a Chinaman which wasn't really suitable, but as luck would have it I ran into Hector Bellville in the bar as both of us had arrived rather early, and he was frightfully steamed up about the Olympics. Wasn't it a bit rich for the Russians to be practising all their general ghastliness and at the same time telling us that it's verboten for the All Black And Tans or whatever they're called — I can never remember which are ours and which are the Kiwis' — to go out to South Africa and kick the ball about with Brother Boer.

By about seven when the others arrived I felt pretty strongly on this issue and after a dozen or so glasses of plonk accompanying whatever it was we were given to toy with over dinner, I was raring to go. Honestly, Bill, I really believed I was on home ground. And judging by the ovation I got from the comrades and the odd bread roll flying through the air I formed the impression I'd gone down rather well. Some silly bugger wrapped himself up in the tablecloth afterwards, occasioning a certain *froideur* from the Toastmaster, but otherwise the horseplay was very mild and a good time was had by all — or so I thought.

Imagine my feelings when I was having one for the road in a little broom cupboard with Hercot and Co afterwards, when the garden centre fellow came creeping up, laid a hand around my shoulders and said he'd been so bowled over by my harangue that he'd taken the liberty of ringing up a friend of his on *The Times*, and that the chap had been absolutely cock-a-hoop, high time somebody spoke up, my views would reach a wider audience etc.

The memory of breakfast next morning is still too painful to be raked over in full: suffice it to say that the decibel counter shot right off the dial. Did I realise that Africa was an unexploded bomb and that I was jumping up and down on it in hobnailed boots, or words to that effect. I said nothing, and at the first lull in the firing put down smoke and retired upstairs to do my devotions. Eric was very decent. He came up after me looking very shaken and said would I like to spend a few days with him and his mother.

In view of this little misunderstanding, I deemed it prudent not to put my oar in on the Affaire Soames — though, to my mind, Bill, Carrington and the Boss are in the rough without a mashie on this one. Soames is a perfectly nice chap, but as I was saying to Boris, can he stand the excitement? You'd never guess it from looking at him, but he's already had one very nasty brush with the Reaper, brought on, I surmise, by over-

51

doing it in Brussels on all fronts, not but what he still remains a doughty quaffer of the snorts, presumably on the grounds, though I haven't taxed him on this, that if you've got to go you've got to go. All very well in Sloane Square, Bill, but what happens when a Fuzzy-Wuzzy jumps out from behind a bush, as occurred when I myself was playing golf with the D of E in Lusaka, waving an assegai and shouting "Whoah ho ho!" or words to that effect?

It's exactly the same as bloody Ulster. Before we know where we are, Bill, we'll be bogged down in Coonsville just like the Frogs at Dien Bien Phu, to general international hilarity on all sides. It just peeves me that thanks to some bloody little garden centre wallah from Maidstone I am going to be held responsible for it.

If I don't see you before, the merriest of Christmasses to you and yours, and don't do anything I wouldn't do.

Yours,

DENIS

Chequers

Dear Bill,

You must think I'm an absolute four-letter fellow for letting you and Daphne down over the Boxing Day tinctures, but *force majeure* intervened yet again. I sent you a p.c. to explain the last-minute change of plan but I imagine you won't have got it. In our neck of the woods we haven't had a delivery or collection as far as I can see for the last fortnight apart from the buff envelopes from the GPO threatening one with death by a thousand cuts. If you ask me, the whole so-called workforce have now got it into their Neanderthal skulls that they are entitled to a month's free holiday over Christmas and the New Year. What it means in real terms is that people like you and me, Bill, are forced to sit on our backsides doing absolutely sod-all when we could be usefully employed.

Everything was reasonably under control until Boxing Day morning, when young Mark, the son and heir, who had to my profound relief failed to respond to his mother's unambiguous directives to join us over the festive board, drove in unannounced in one of his souped-up BRMs, knocking over two of the Elizabethan bollards planted outside this monstrosity by one of the former incumbents. At his side, need I say, a very solid looking air-hostess from Air Danske with whom, it seemed, he had struck up an acquaintance on one of their scheduled flights. His mother had been up working for some three or four hours in the Baldwin Room, so I was obliged, if you please, to bustle down and play mine genial host.

God, Bill, what a ballsacher! Great Dane entirely mute, refusing all refreshment, prodigal son full of interminable anecdotes re his latest business venture viz advertising felt-tip pens on his bloody racing car. All the time, I must say, stuffing his face with a massive fry-up very decently conjured into existence out of hours by Mr Wu, the Filipino custodian in the employ of the National Trust, which quite put me off my first snort of the day. I was about to recommend a wash and brush up prior to his being received into the maternal bosom when M. anticipated my thoughts by sweeping in, dressed to the nines and muttering about Afghanistan. I could see at a glance that she was slightly less than delighted by the scene that met her eyes, particularly when Miss Piggy failed to respond in any way, staring sulkily at her shoes and gripping her Air Danske travelling bag. I thought it prudent at this point to toddle off, feeling as I always do rather defenceless in a dressing-gown and slippers.

While slipping into the tweeds, I discovered from Boris — he, lucky man, was able to spend Christmas entirely alone in the attic — that some celebration was afoot, and we were entertaining the Carringtons to lunch. My spirits couldn't have been much lower, but I realised on arriving in what passes for the drawing-room that things were more disastrous than even I had feared. Mr Wu had failed to clear away the little red ropes that normally keep the public off the furniture, and the central heating had packed it in a few hours earlier. It's always pretty chilly in this ghastly mausoleum even when it works, and by now you could see your breath.

The Danish Bacon was still in situ: it seemed that Mark had put in a word on social poise, and the sulky expression had given way to a glassy and immutable smile. All Peter Carrington's very remarkable powers of diplomacy, successful though they may have been with the Coons, seemed to be making little impact on the Anglo-Danish front. Doubles seemed to be in order. Lady Carrington, who is really a very good sport, got down on her hands and knees in the grate and tried to get a fire going out of some old National Trust literature and a model of *Morning Cloud* left behind by Heath. Mark meanwhile had done something to appease the maternal wrath by producing a presentation hamper from Harrods, now enshrined in the place of honour under the Christmas tree.

Lunch, in our overcoats, was not the happiest of occasions, and Mr Wu's curried turkey croquettes were by no means the success they might have been. For long periods there was no sound but the clink of cutlery on plates, and curious looks were exchanged between M. and the Danish Blue. After Mr Wu, now in a mood of suppressed hysteria, had handed round the cold Christmas pud and we had drained four bottles of very decent Chateau Talbot out of the cellar, Mark volunteered to

54

burrow underneath the tree, and came back with a huge box of Harrods' Al Koran Drambuie-Filled Chocolate Bonbons. "Here you are, Ma" — pushing them in her face — "your favourites", at which a carbon-copy invoice fluttered into M's lap, clearly made out to "Mrs M. Thatcher" of Downing Street for 250 nicker, overprinted with a red rubber stamp expressing hopes of an early settlement of the account.

As you know, Bill, I am always an optimist. I had hoped that M. would restrain her feelings at least until the departure of our guests, but I was wrong and we were instantly bent to ground level in the fury of a real Force-Eighter. Thank God for Boris and the little billiard-room-cum-cocktail-lounge under the roof, installed by the Lady Falkender for her personal researches.

On a warmer note, I've been looking through some of these holiday brochures. If Daphne's wanderlust is still unabated, how about you and me sampling the Off Season Duty-Free on the Isola d'Elba? A magnificent new 18-holer, all mod cons, six days from £299.73.

Vive le Sport.

Yours till the cows come home,

DENIS

10 Downing Street
Whitehall

Dear Bill,

I hope this catches you before you and Daphne embus for Gatwick. I must say the Barbados Package sounds like a lot of fun. I met a chap in the Club the other day who had just come back from Kowloon, which I believe is somewhere in that neck of the woods, and he said the Duty-Free was flowing like water, but on no account to touch the seafood. I must confess to a pang on opening your missive. I could just see you and I sitting out on the little wrought-iron balcony in the brochure in our bibs and tuckers with the dusky hostess bearing down on us in her lua lua with a couple of triple Snortos de Luxe. But ah me, as it is, London W.C. will have to be my lot.

I must say the news as the year begins is enough to make one embark on the bare bodkin routine. M. is frightfully steamed up about the Russian Bear. Quite right too in my book. Boris of course is biased on this one, but as one who knows his Burma and has seen Johnny Gurkha on the job, I see the whole thing as crystal-clear. Peter Carrington dropped in the other night with his missus for a bite. A very nice chap, no side at all, told me he *did* remember Sticky at Eton, but more of that anon when we meet. Lady C. is an absolute brick, and while she and M. went off to powder their noses I took the opportunity of putting in my two-pennyworth. As I told him, with the help of the very serviceable *Reader's Digest World Atlas and Restaurant Guide* your Tunbridge Wells friend kindly slipped into my arms after that shindig at the Pantiles, Warm Water Ports is the name of the game. Ever since the days of Ivan the Terrible, I explained over a tincture or twain, what the Russky has always craved is somewhere to keep his fleet where it isn't too cold. Archangel and so forth often frozen up about Christmas time. What more natural then than for the Red Menace to come rolling through the Khyber, next stop

Colombo, and there's your W.W.P?

Carrington seemed very receptive to my little geography lesson, which I hope provided a salutary antidote to what he gets fed by the assorted Moles, Pinkoes and Wooftahs at the F.O. As he did not reply in so many words, merely drumming his fingers on the tabletop and looking at the ceiling — always a sign in my experience that the little grey cells are working flat out — I was emboldened to propose something short and sharp. No earthly use, I ventured to suggest, in buggering about banning the export of breakfast cereals, they can always fill up with lentils. Withdrawing our show-jumping team from the Olympic Caper seems equally pointless, pissing in the wind, only leave the way open for the Japs to nab all the silver pots and trophies. Far better a quick blitz with half a dozen ICBMs, only language these chaps understand. Witness A. Hitler, failure to deal with menace of.

I could see Carrington absorbing all this, eyes tightly closed in concentration. However, when we joined the Boss and Lady C. for the After Eights, the conversation turned to the rights and wrongs of index-linked perks for non-residential ex-industrialists. I now learn that as far as the Red Menace is concerned there are plans afoot to cancel the forthcoming visit of the Leningrad Formation Ice-Skating Team. That'll stop the Mongol Hordes in their tracks, eh Bill? Poor old Colombo is all I have to add.

Perhaps you detect a note of cynicism creeping in. I found myself in the lift at Number Ten the other day with old Howe. I don't know if you remember him: glasses, brothel-creepers, quite a decent bird in the main but hardly one for a night of mischief at the Pig & Whistle. He seemed to think, poor jerk, that I had some influence with M., and weighed in on the steel strike. As you know, M's line on this is the Three Wise Monkey Gambit — not the Government's baby, let the buggers fight it out among themselves and so forth. Howe seemed to have got it into his head that it *was* somehow the Government's responsibility in view of the fact that the Government was actually the employer and would have to foot the bill, whatever they decide. Quite a sound point, Bill, I think you'll agree.

However the Boss is not, as you know, over-open to persuasion. I told Howe that as a married man he ought to know that when dealing with the fair sex the only option open is to sit on arse, keep head down and wait for wind to change:

not then to be too surprised, when this happens, if your point of view is claimed to have been hers all along.

So, if you ask me, little Len Murray will be toddling round for a tincture within the very foreseeable future.

The Major has opened a book on the Fatty In Coonsville saga. I've given him evens on our portly friend having to be winched out by helicopter as the blood rises around his knees. However, let's hope for everyone's sake that they can patch up some sort of semblance of a settlement and get the hell out of it before that scenario actually goes into production.

Give my regards to civilisation when you get there, and bring me back a bottle of that 200-proof if you have room in your little zip-bag.

Yours, holding the fort,

DENIS

---

10 Downing Street
Whitehall

1 FEBRUARY 1980

Dear Bill,

Ta for the p.c., which, alas, was not received at our breakfast table with quite the mirth I'm sure you intended. Boris insisted on showing it to M., hoping to curry favour, and her response was grim in the extreme. Would I kindly see to it in future that if my golfing friends wish to send obscene material through the post they do so in a sealed package. Quite enough trouble as it was without giving the Press another stick to beat us with. Nil desperandum, however. Boris and I found the dusky lady absolutely irresistible, and have got her propped up on the mantelpiece in our little den in the attic.

The Boss is over the moon with the War Fever. I must say I am all in favour of buggering up the Olympics. For a start it always occupies the TV to the exclusion of better things, e.g. Angela Rippon and *Pot Black*, and then again, what's the point

of a huge jamboree like that if it excludes the only decent game, and indeed one of the oldest, ever invented? So full marks to the Boss for her firm stand in Round One. I did opine, over a Twiglet, that the idea of putting the whole bang-shoot into Olympia seemed a bit outre. Those sort of places are always booked up months in advance anyway with DIY conventions, Health Food weirdoes and Caravan Shows, as the Major discovered when he and Picarda had that wheeze for flogging the cargo of reject Japanese greenhouses to the unsuspecting populace.

The Boss however would hear none of it, and poor little Cosgrove had to ring round every Bingo Hall and Greyhound Stadium in the country and ask if they had any cancellations. Result: no can do all round. My proposal for International Golfing Tournament sponsored by one of the big snort merchants instantly vetoed.

Ding, Ding, Round Two. Various elderly Senior Citizens summoned round. From their appearance in the hall I took them to be a British Legion delegation whose home had fallen under the axe, come to plead for mercy. Not so. Every one of the old buffers had at some time twinkled round the track bearing the Olympic Torch. Frogmarched en masse into Boss's sanctum, yours truly roped in to pass round warm sherry, M. sweeps in giving her Virgin Queen, reads them all the Riot Act, no truckling to Russian Bear or Government rug pulled from under young Gymnasts in no uncertain manner. At this, one cherry-nosed old party having trouble with his hearing-aid made point that they were all booked into Moscow Hilton, whole caper insured at Lloyds fifty-six million pounds, loss in souvenirs alone would bankrupt country, and anyway Hitler not such a bad fellow, made trains run on time. No wonder the Boss got nowhere. Cherry-nosed party blows noisily through pipe, unaware of Gorgon glance which would have turned anyone more alert to stone. Cosgrove told me old codger won a bronze for hop skip and jump in 1911. Incredible, isn't it?

Only decent chuckle material we've had was provided by M's creepy little chum Stevarse. All of us here, or Boris at least, knew perfectly well the Budget was going to clash with the Enthronement highjinks at Canterbury. Indeed, when the thing originally cropped up, Howe sought me out personally for a gut reaction. What would be drinking man's view? With a flash of insight I suggested double-booking: with two functions on same day any reasonable man can get out of both by saying he's at the other one. Howe agreed, observing that three hours amid the flowered hats in Canterbury Cathedral listening to *Hymns A&M* not his idea of bliss. I omitted to counter that a similar period locked in the Distinguished Strangers' Pen wearing the Moss Bros. bib and tucker listening to him drooling on over the little red box not exactly mine.

All would have been hunky-dory had it not been for our friend Stevarse who came mincing round reeking of garlic after a troughful of Risotto with our iceycreamio chums Saatchi and Saatchi. I spotted he was up to something from the way he was wringing his hands like a sky-pilot on the make. "What an opportunity", he tells the Boss, all misty-eyed, "to show that spiritual values not dead, religion meaningful role to play in the Eighties, Ayatollah not entirely barking up wrong tree, materialism on the run etc." Quite honestly, Bill, it made me feel sick. But as you know, the Boss took a shine to Stevarse from the start — God knows why. Clear as the balls on a dog the man's an A1 bumsucker. So you can cross March 25th and March 26th off the map as far as I'm concerned.

Give my regards to Mrs Nightingale at the Lamb & Flag and ask her if she still remembers the night we played Spud-arse along the top of the Saloon Bar after Rollo Whittaker's funeral.

Yours in the Lord,

DENIS

Study this!

Chequers

DIPLOMATIC ETIQUETTE

Dear Bill,

Glad to hear you and Daphne are back on terra firma and, according to the Major, black as a couple of coons. It must be a touch disheartening to find so little changed during your absence, i.e. pickets at every corner baying defiance, and a bill for £25 when you fill up the limo. Personally I have decided to put the Rolls into mothballs and keep it exclusively for trade-in purposes.

The Major managed to get through the minefield the other night, ringing me up to ask what the hell was going on. I had to say that quite honestly I hadn't the faintest clue. I myself am rapidly approaching the stage where I couldn't give a bugger anyway.

A propos the Steel Strike, we had all been led to suppose that Mr Sirs and his merry men were going to be thrashed to the ground with knouts pour encourager les autres as Napoleon put it, and not a moment too soon in my humble estimation. I even risked entering the Boss's bedroom the other night to lend support, venturing the view as she laboured with her curlers that sooner or later the peasants were going to have to be whipped into line, even if it meant giving them a bloody nose in the process, and why not start on poor old Sirs, who seems to me quite a decent chap and therefore more likely to tug his forelock and withdraw after such an encounter. The Red Robbo brigade made of sterner stuff etc. M. nodded and asked me to be sure to turn out the light on the landing.

Next morning, imagine my surprise, on abandoning the crossword after a damn good stab, to see on page one of the *D. Tel.* that Sirs was about to be bought off to the tune of 22%. Quite obviously the Have A Go faction had been nobbled, and Villiers had caved in. I tried to catch M's eye over breakfast, but without success. As Boris was helping her on with her boots, however, she did observe that it was nothing to do with the Government. Christ Almighty, Bill, it makes me want to take a mashie niblick and get in amongst them myself. On reading the small print, it would appear as follows:

Plan A: No money in kitty, and such as there was to be doled out in the form of putty handshakes to redundant members of so-called workforce. Plan collapses.

Plan B: Forget Plan A. Hand out redundancy money in form of cash bonanza. Just imagine, Bill, if we'd done that sort of thing in the Boardroom at Burmah! Boris informs me that the new scenario is to forget whole episode, bringing in New Legislation to stop it happening again.

Who, you might ask, Bill, is behind this ongoing balls-up? None other than our old friend Sir Keith Joseph, Svengali, the Mad Monk, assisted by friend Howe, who, I am beginning to opine, has very little going on between the ears. So, according to the latest bulletin, it's full steam ahead now for New Laws. Pickets illegal, proles absolutely at liberty to strike providing no inconvenience caused.

Last Tuesday evening I happened to stumble on the Monk spelling out this latest lunacy to the Boss over a lotion in her little sitting-room upstairs. You should see him in action, Bill: it's quite a sight. Eyes rolling, fingers scratching at the roots of his curly locks, then leaping up, and pacing about overturning everything that isn't nailed to the floor. Rather like that peculiar brother of Maurice Picarda's who set up as a shrink in Bournemouth. (Wasn't he struck off?) M. watches, teeth agleam, eyes filled with admiration, rabbit hypnotised by snake syndrome. I was helping myself to a large brownie from the lotion cupboard and doing my best to keep the blood pressure normal. However, when he paused for breath I decided to put my oar in. All very well wheeling out the senile beaks like Gaffer Denning: what if revolutionary mob raises two fingers? My query was obviously seen as only an irritation. The Bold Baronet muttered something about crossing that bridge, fullness of time, majority of unions law-abiding etc. Boss looking firmly at toe-cap, jaw set. Yours truly ploughs on with history lesson. E. Heath, Industrial Relations Court, Pentonville Martyrs. Our Lot made to look bloody idiots.

Silly of me as it turned out. Always unwise to refer to M's sea-faring predecessor. Solids hit airconditioning in no uncertain manner. Anything that went wrong that time all Heath's fault, my views irrelevant and unwished for, yours truly there to be

seen but not heard, ideally neither.

I did have a quiet word with Jim Prior however by the back door, and he said he thought the Monk was due for a spell in the funny farm. Apparently, during their meeting, though this is absolutely for your ears only, Prior enquired what happened if there was a General Strike? Cannot arrest whole population. Not enough bobbies to go round. Joseph's solution: recruit more bobbies. I ask you, Bill! Not that the Monk's legislation will ever come to pass in any shape or form, but it does make you yearn for the old days of Peterloo and so forth, when they knew how to do these things.

Oh, by the way, Boris is fairly certain that the Special Branch are listening in on our phone calls. Apparently, thanks to this new micro-chip technology, certain keywords will start the spools going round in their cellar. So don't be too surprised if you find my conversation somewhat guarded. The Major was very mystified, particularly by the noise of Boris clattering about with his de-bugging kit. However, the following code will apply in future: The Boss equals "Ethel". The Major equals "our mutual friend". Golf equals "Boardroom meeting". This should do for a start. See you at the Driving Range on Friday and ask Mrs Ferguson to line them up at the bar. It is my intention to get really plastered.

Your old chum,

DENIS

---

10 Downing Street
Whitehall

29 FEBRUARY 1980

Dear Bill,

Sorry to be a bit short on the phone. I knew perfectly well what you wanted to know, but with the Boss in a dudgeon at my elbow my replies had perforce to be somewhat clipped. All I can say is that it hasn't been entirely disagreeable to see another member of the family, to wit the son and heir, taking it in the neck for a change.

As you know, Bill, Mark and I have never exactly hit it off. I could have overlooked his chucking golf lessons after only two sessions on the links, but when he used the set of half-size clubs from Hamleys I gave him for his seventh birthday to light the bonfire with I realised that we would have to go our separate ways. Nothing he has done since has ever given me cause to revise my opinion. Still, there it is. New wine and old bottles, as somebody said. As for bringing the little bugger to heel, I long since banished that idea from the realm of possibility. Not that his mother's ever had a great deal of time for him either, between ourselves, though she did kick up a bit rough when he started on this Fangio business in the first place. Quite understandable in the circs: animal instinct to preserve our young. Even though the sight of the little swine makes one want to puke, one doesn't like the thought of him going over the hard shoulder and snuffing it in a blaze of publicity.

I remember at the time I was detailed to have a man-to-man chinwag about it all and try to steer his thoughts into dress-designing or accountancy. Needless to say, the whole exercise was a non-event. He just sat there with a sulky sort of look sipping his rum and coca-cola and inferring that I was some sort of alcoholic idiot spending the twilight of my life staggering from green to green with various derelicts and deadbeats. Some truth in it, I suppose, if I am to be perfectly honest, but I was buggered if I was going to take it from a long-haired spotty-faced whippersnapper like that who doesn't know his arse from his elbow.

Anyway after that I took the view that as far as I was concerned he could go to hell in a handcart. He was fairly hard put to it to do a three-point turn in any case, so no one seemed very anxious to come up with the spondulicks. Even the rubber johnny merchants gave him the thumbs down, and you couldn't go much lower than that, eh? (I must say, even I would have qualms about allowing my first-born to hurtle round Brands Hatch at a hundred mph flogging french letters to the great unwashed.)

I was therefore not displeased when old Eric, my body-guard, who usually toddles down to the corner to pick up the evening edition, showed me the item about this big Jap conglomerate Phuwhatascorcha Co. offering to put something up front in return for him modelling their electrically-heated

rain-hats. I said to Boris, "He could do a lot worse than that." Besides which, it did cross my mind that there might be the odd free trip for yours truly to the Land of the Rising Sun where, as you know, if the Major is to be believed, there are many avenues to be explored by the fun-loving golf enthusiast and *bon viveur*. (Not a word to Bessie etc!) M. didn't seem too miffed at the time, it being no great loss, in her view, were young Mark to be permanently exported to Japan and points East.

As usual, all would have been well had it not been for the filthy reptiles of Fleet Street. Before you could say Red Robbo every jumped-up dirty-necked little leader-writer was sniggering away about the Japanese Connection, Pissing on the Flag, what's wrong with British electrically-heated rain-hats and so forth, conveniently forgetting that no self-respecting British company would touch the little bugger with a bargepole. Labour mob up on their feet like a pack of monkeys at the zoo, pelting the Boss with anything they can lay their hands on. Proprietor inevitably displeased. I am summoned to the Snug, nicely woozy on Boris's vodka, to do my heavy father bit. Helter-skelter to Flood Street, Boris at the wheel, enter over back wall to avoid press, tear new pair of cavalry twill trousers from arsehole to breakfast table, finally track down son and h. slouched in front of TV amid litter of beer cans.

To my amazement, immediate cave-in on all fronts. No question of embracing Nips if M. doesn't like it, has British sponsor up sleeve. It occurred to me on the way back to the Lubjanka there might be a catch in it, and indeed there was. Next thing we know Mark emerging from Massage Parlour to maximum publicity brandishing offers from some seedy Soho tit-and-bum wallah who publishes *Men Only* in his spare time. I don't know if you've seen *Men Only* recently, Bill, but it has rather changed since the days when you and I would peruse a dog-eared black-and-white copy in the Mess over a snort or two. I sent Eric down to W.H. Smith to pick up a sample but what he found within clearly distressed the poor old boy terribly. I'm a broad-minded chap myself, Bill, as you know, but some of the material puts one in mind of old Army days doing a Clap Round on the Reeperbahn. Moments later, Mark on the phone. "Okay? Hope M. is now satisfied, real bunk-up for British magazine publishing. Soho Johnny nice bloke, anxious to come round for a snifter at Number Ten."

Result inevitable. No official intervention from M. Mark agrees to sever connections with porn-wallah, future silence assured in exchange re-opening unlimited credit facilities M's account Harrods, Man About Town Tailoring Company, Talbot Winemart etc. Don't say the Young Tories don't know their 'A' level Economics.

Looks as if Villiers is for the high-jump. Only problem, no one will take the job. I have suggested Maurice Picarda. Not the most scrupulous of men, I agree, but a staunch Conservative and not an utter prat like Villiers.

Yours very affectionately,

DENIS

---

10 Downing Street
Whitehall

14 MARCH 1980

Dear Bill,

Hats off to Fatty Soames. I must say he fooled me. There was a time, as you know, when Boris and I were absolutely at one in thinking the old boy would be winched out by a chopper as the blood rose over his knees. As it is, the stage seems well and truly set for our overweight chum to climb into his feathered hat and watch the flag pulled down with a modicum of dignity. The D of E rang to say he was under some pressure from the better half to turn out for the Last Post but that he was, entre nous, resisting it. His plan now is to try and winkle out one of the younger generation to go and stand in on behalf of the Great White Mother Across The Sea.

I find the whole thing extraordinarily puzzling, Bill. After all, we had been led to suppose that this Mugabe character was the devil incarnate, hands steeped in gore, loincloth laden down with Moscow gold etc. etc. so I was a bit nonplussed when little Carrington came bouncing in rubbing his hands and saying everything was tickety-boo. I could see at once that the Boss didn't share his enthusiasm, so I suggested to our noble friend that a lotion might not come amiss. A generous brownie and soda made his eyes gleam somewhat, and he raised the Waterford crystal to remark, "Well, Prime Minister, here's to the new Democratic People's Republic of Zimbabwe!" He then drained the tumbler, while the Boss continued to give him one of her looks. "I thought, Peter," she said, in a frosty-ish tone, "our money was on the Bishop." "But don't you see?" the modern Metternich exclaimed, extending his glass for a refill, "that's what it's all about, Baby Doll. Free and Fair Elections! May the best man win!" It crossed my mind at this point that he might have had one or two before he arrived — some kind of FO celebration. M. however remained unmoved. "I don't like it one little bit," she said. "Kindly make it clear to him that one step out of line and he will get it very hard over the knuckles." Carrington wisely refrained at this juncture from pursuing the point further, and turned the conversation to events nearer home.

I took the liberty of pouring a little cold water over Carrington myself on the way out to the lift. I don't know if you know, but the Major's brother Clem who went off to Rhodesia after the 39-45 show and did very well out of copper sulphate has been making noises for some time about catching the first plane out, and now that Comrade Mugabe has assumed the reins of office I imagine he'll be over any minute. The point I put to Peter Carrington is that they're obviously not going to be able to run the country without the Major's brother and his ilk, so he shouldn't be too cock-a-hoop. I formed the impression, as he got into the lift with some difficulty, that he frankly didn't give a bugger. "Well," he shouted, as the doors began to close, "it's not my responsibility now, chum! Get the British bobbies back, and if all the suburban riff-raff who went out to feather their beastly little nests get chopped up into tiny bits by the natives, I personally shall not lift a finger to prevent it." With this the doors closed, the lift lurched downwards and he sank, swaying, out of sight.

I must say, Bill, I was a bit shocked by his attitude. I went straight back upstairs, opened another bottle, and wrote a firm note to Carrington suggesting the moment Clem hits Gatwick we should all get together at the Army & Navy and give him the benefit of a view from the grass roots.

Gilmour and Carrington are all very well in their way, but, like Sticky, they tend to take a rather lofty view of things. What else? Oh yes, ambitious brother Howe is busy preparing his Budget. Boris always has his ear to the ground and tells me that booze and fags are a cert — talk of a ten per cent rise! — and that one of us should get round to the Cash & Carry before the 25th. Could you have a word with your pal Hoddinott who runs the Clubhouse to fix me up with a dozen crates of each and about 200 cartons of anything in the Middle Tar bracket to see me through to summer? Boris says the saving should be very considerable.

Something cf a flutter in the henhouse right now about the bye-election at Southend East. Saatchi & Saatchi are in and out with their charts and tables from morning to night making fatuous suggestions — "Realism" is the hard sell, whatever that means. I told M. they could start off by getting a decent candidate. What price the Major's brother?

Yours pro tem,

DENIS

10 Downing Street
Whitehall

28 MARCH 1980

Dear Bill,

Stroll on, what a week! I don't know whether you've ever been to an Enthronement, but I would strongly advise against it. The charabanc left Downing Street at some Godforsaken hour, very depressing drive through the East End, bloody cold to boot, and M. plainly narked at being called away from affairs of State. Eric insisted on sitting in the front so as to take the first impact of any assassination attempt, and I was stuck in the back between Boris and the Boss. As B. is on the bulky side you can imagine I emerged somewhat crushed outside the Archiepiscopal digs. Needless to say, we were early. The Boss always has to leave two hours in case of punctures, acts of God, earthquakes etc.

You know the form at these sky-pilots' get-togethers — remember the grisly evening we once spent with the Bishop of

Deal the time he blessed the Golf Course, silly bugger? (Who's daft idea was that?) I knew perfectly well that all we were going to get while we were kicking our heels was a thick glass of warm cooking sherry and as we went through the oaken door I was feeling pretty depressed, I don't mind admitting. Mrs Runcie, reeking of some tarty scent, was doing the honours in a silly hat with fruit on, and Runcie himself was hovering about in a long purple get-up rubbing his hands and showing his teeth. I took the Boss aside and began to tell her she'd picked a wrong 'un and they should have had old Archie Wellbeloved, senile or not senile, but I was sent away with a flea in my ear as per usual and told not to be preposterous.

At this juncture all eyes turned to the door at the arrival of Royalty and the Number Two Seed tottered in looking very merry in a veil. I was just thinking, Bill, what a relief she hadn't brought that frightful little nancy-boy with her when she made a bee-line for me, ignoring the grinning Bish, and led me discreetly into a corner behind the bust of some bearded buffer from Victorian days. "You and I are going to go out into the garden and admire the daffodils," she hissed through clenched teeth, a note of great firmness in her voice, and before I knew it, she had a firm grip on my arm and was steering me through the French windows. Once outside, her manner changed. "God, what a relief," she breathed. "If they think we're going to get through three hours of all that jiggery-pokery without a couple of big ones they must be out of their tiny minds."

I know a cry for help when I hear one, Bill, and in no time at all we had swung a leg over the garden wall, shot down a little cobbled alleyway, and were lining them up in the firelit snug of the Miller's Arms.

Very approachable lady, Bill. Full of good tales, and as you will have gathered from the above, not averse to the odd snort. We managed to take on board half a dozen large G and Ts before a breathless Eric, his tie and raincoat in disarray, burst through the curtain to announce that Stevarse had observed our departure and ratted to the Boss. Would we kindly take our seats as the balloon was going up? I don't remember a great deal of the ceremony. I must have dropped off I think while a whiskery old Greek was saying a word or two on behalf of our sundered brethren in the East. I found it all very confusing. As I said to Princess Margaret, I thought

it was meant to be a CofE beano, and yet the place was swarming with RCs, Methodists and God knows what.

Back at the Barracks I was inevitably called into the study and given a wigging for going AWOL, but fortunately I had the Prerogative to fall back on, Royal Will not to be denied etc. Didn't go down too well, but better than nothing.

A few brief hours of troubled sleep and then back into the bib and tucker for little friend Howe's hour of glory. I have never understood why he can't just get up and say "A quid on fags, couple of quid on petrol etc.", and then sit down again. Instead of which we are treated to a ballsaching lecture before-hand on the state of the nation with special reference to such fascinating topics as International Monetary Trends, Excess Surpluses and Taking Up The Slack. Thank goodness I am beginning to know the ropes. I always choose a seat at the back of the gallery on the gangway, and after a suitable inter-val I get a very nasty frog in the throat, of the type that prevents other members of the audience from catching the jewels being scattered below. Stifling the sounds in vain with a hanky, and amid sympathetic murmurs, I then bang out through the swing doors, and away like the clappers to the House of Lords' Lounge, where there is always a very decent crowd watching the Racing, and even a hot line to Joe Coral's.

Wilson was sitting in a corner looking rather under the weather with a bottle of brandy in one hand and a balloon glass in the other, and I got chatting to him. Quite a decent cove, Bill. Very fond of golf and used an umbrella to show me a wheeze for getting cut of a bunker in the rain with a number three lofting iron. At about five o'clock they started serving tea and cakes, and I asked him what had happened in the Budget, but he said he didn't know and didn't give a bugger. I know you'll find it hard to believe, Bill, but I think he's one of us. One of these days I really feel we ought to invite him down to Littlestone. I'd give a great deal to see the Major's face when we stomp in with his arch-enemy in tow.

As you will see from the *Telegraph*, M's Band of Wets have taken a bit of a thrashing from Howe, but I think he's got absolutely the right idea. High time some of these unemployed layabouts started paying for the pleasures of those of us who do a bit of work. All best to Daphne. Wrap up well.

Yours,

DENIS

Chequers

Dear Bill,

I'm sorry Hoddinott was so miffed about the liquor run to Number Ten. Tell him I'll see him right with a couple of blueys next time I'm down at Worplesdon. My fault entirely. I should have explained about bringing it round the back. As it was I gather he started lugging crates out of his hatchback bang outside the front door on Budget Eve and all the tourists began to cheer. Thinking there was some pro-Tory demo organised by Saatchi & Saatchi afoot, M. stuck her head out of the first-floor window to acknowledge the greetings of the Faithful, and there's poor old H. struggling to get his arms round a Europack of litre-size Mother's Ruin. We were definitely not amused.

H. got a flea in his ear before being duffed up by the Special Patrol Unit, always on the lurk with weighted truncheons looking for a spot of fun. I hurried down to try and rescue the booze at least, but every bloody bottle had already been impounded by the Commissioner, and all I got was six of the best from the Boss, and three days in Coventry.

A propos the Budget, the general consensus at the watering holes would appear to be that our lawyer friend Howe could have done a damn sight worse. I had a word with Mine Host at the Waggonload of Monkeys in Great Missenden, and his view was that it was high time somebody got a grip on the strikers and came down on their free hand-outs and that anyone who was prepared to go out and give the so-called workers a good solid boot in the balls had his vote. A bit extreme, you may think, but I find more and more of our sort talking in that vein on my whistle-stop tours of the local hostelries.

By the way, Bill, you might be interested to hear that Howe very sensibly consulted me as part of his grass roots soundings before toddling down Mount Sinai with his battered old bag. We found ourselves sitting next to each other at one of those ghastly receptions for some visiting potentate at the Fishmongers' Hall and he asked me would I go white about the gills if he slammed fifty pee on a bottle of snorts. I spotted his drift at once. Obviously the mandarins had got the wind up at the last minute: drinking man's backlash, heels dug in, con-

sumption peaks off, etc. By way of reply I recalled the case of that old sawbones who was always propping up the bar at Rye. Furnival? Bulstrode? Anyway I think he turned his toes up a few years ago after a prolonged period of St Vitus Dance and DTs. (I always remember M. used to object to the fumes when he was feeling her chest in a professional capacity.)

Anyway, one Budget night I shall never forget, old Venables or whatever his name was banged on the bar with his knob-kerry and announced to all and sundry that enough was enough. In protest at yet another imposition by the Chancellor he wanted everyone to witness that he was about to sink his final snort this side of the grave. He then filled a beermug with Stag's Breath, drained the lot, and was duly carried out by some of his medical chums who knew the form. But, as I said to Howe, and this was the point, precisely three nights later there he was back on his stool, looking like death warmed up and paying his surcharge like the rest of us.

Howe obviously got the message. Not that I'm in favour of it, you understand, Bill, but as I said to Boris, what's fifty pee nowadays? Give it to the cloakroom wallah at the Savoy and he'll spit in your eye.

Talking of money, you'll have seen that that stupid arse Villiers has surrendered to the Steel Coolies, precisely as I predicted he would bloody months back. After all the talk of only two per cent and taking a firm stand, hey presto, what does he do but mill about for months on end and then collapse. I made this point to M. at breakfast, and expressed the thought to no one in particular that no doubt they would be throwing in a free Savile Row suit and holidays in the South of France. Eric, my bodyguard, sniggered a bit into his cornflakes but he got one of M's black looks and soon stopped.

A quiet Easter in the main. Mark, thank the Lord, has gone off to practise his reversing and three-point turns at a disused airport somewhere near Kidderminster. M. had that smarmy bloke from Brussels, Jenkins, down to chew the fat vis a vis our European Contributions, and the only excitement came when Wilson, who has a little hideyhole just up the road from here, rang up during the Boat Race to propose a round of golf with some Lebanese friends of his on Bank Holiday Monday. Needless to say, M. put the kibosh on this "for security reasons". What she means is the Press might get hold of it, further ridicule and contempt etc. for fraternising with the other side, even though Wilson himself hates the Unions as much as you or me, and told me in strict confidence that that secretary of his there was all the trouble about actually voted for our side last time round.

Ah well, see you at the Reunion on the 14th.

Yours aye,

DENIS

10 Downing Street
Whitehall
25 APRIL 1980

Dear Bill,

Sorry I couldn't make the Reunion. For once the coast was clear on the Proprietor front, but bloody Boris had been tinkering with the Rolls all weekend and when it came to the count-down she spluttered a bit and then conked out. All done up in my bib and tucker, juices going nicely at the thought of snorts to come, and the old girl dies on me. Boris crawled underneath, followed by yours truly, in a bit of a temper by this time, but no joy. Next train wouldn't have got me down till after midnight, limos all tied up, Mr Patel of the minicabs celebrating Pakistani New Year. I rang through to the Lady Hamilton Suite at the Anchor but as usual only got some Filipino cove with a very limited grasp of the language. In the end Boris and I mooched off in the direction of the bright lights, v. down at heart, and after one or two scrapes ended up in some refurbished Georgian joint in Mayfair with a lot of sweaty Arabs throwing their money away as if there was no tomorrow.

Talking of Arabs, I thought Peter Carrington went a bit far grovelling to the Chief Wog about the TV knees-up. I told him so myself when he dropped in for a hamburger and a glass of port conjured up by the Boss for the Salisbury briefing. He said he hated doing it, but the Children of Allah v. touchy and there was a lot of money involved. I suppose it makes sense though honestly, when you think of the way we used to handle the buggers in Benghazi it's jolly weird I think you'll agree...
Do you remember the night the Colonel squirted the fire extinguisher all over the dhobi wallah? Through the window like a dose of salts, as I recall. No apologies on that occasion.

Meanwhile we're all supposed to be getting steamed up about the Hostages. The Boss, as you may have noticed, is v. carried away, everything within our power to support friend Carter in his hour of need etc. Sanctions, naval blockade, threat of nuclear bombardment. Fortunately I managed to get my oar in before everybody went quite over the top. Carrington, as I think I've told you, is a very approachable geezer, and I

79

broached matters with him when we found ourselves shoulder-to-shoulder in the downstairs gents at Number Ten.

My theme, Bill, was this. You and I know brother Wog and what an excitable little chap he is. Threaten him with a big stick and the danger is that before you can say knife you'll have him whirling like a dervish, eyes flashing fire, bonfire of American flags blazing away on every side, situation v. disagreeable. The other point I pressed home on our friend, who very decently agreed to follow me up to the boxroom for a nocturnal lotion, was that trying to impose sanctions was about as much good as flogging rubber johnnies in a monastery. You try and stop the Japs, for instance, piling in, all spectacles and flashing gold teeth, if they sniff a market for their motor-bikes and electric xylophones. Ditto the Frog. Ditto practically everyone you can think of, viz BP in Rhodesia.

Replenishing our friend's toothmug with another generous shot of the duty-free, I made my third point — in my view the clincher. All very well for Carter to ask everyone to rally round for his Middle Eastern adventures, but what happened at Suez? In we go, grin grin from Uncle Sam, shit hits fan and you can't see the buggers for dust. In plain man's language, you've got to watch the Yanks in the rough.

Carrington seemed very receptive, I must say, to all of the above. What's more, he agreed with me wholeheartedly as we negotiated our way down the stairs from the attic that there's something bloody rum about a bloke of Carter's age going round holding hands with his wife in public.

Neither of us had any idea it was so late, but when I attempted to unravel the various chains and bolts on the front door, imagine my surprise when the burglar alarm system went off with the noise of fifty fire-engines going flat out. Eric was first down the pole, cloth cap and dressing-gown with Luger at the ready, what a prize ass that man is, closely followed by the Boss, hair in curlers, poker in hand, eyes flashing killer rays. Carrington's powers of diplomacy enabled him to shimmer through the crack unharmed, leaving yours truly to take it in the neck as per usual.

By the bye. Did you see that fellow Mugabe going on about being in love with Fatty Soames? Is it me, Bill, or is everyone going completely barmy?

Yours to the death,

DENIS